# PAST, PRESENT, FUTURE

## Stories that Haunt

# DR. IAN PRATTIS

Manor House

# Library and Archives Canada
# Cataloguing in Publication

Title: Past, present, future : stories that haunt / Dr. Ian Prattis.

Names: Prattis, J. I., author.

Description: Short stories and essays.

Identifiers: Canadiana 20210160861 |

ISBN 9781988058665 (hardcover) |

ISBN 9781988058672 (softcover)

Classification: LCC PS8631.R396 P37 2021 | DDC C813/.6—dc23

Front Cover art: Sira Anamwong / Shutterstock / (Silhouettes of unidentified tourists looking through clock with roman numerals in the museum D'Orsay).
Back Cover art: Carolyn Hill (photo of the Author)

First Edition
Cover Design-layout / Interior- layout: Michael Davie
192 pages  /  46,827 words.  All rights reserved.
Published 2021  /  Copyright 2021
Manor House Publishing Inc.
452 Cottingham Crescent, Ancaster, ON, L9G 3V6
www.manor-house-publishing.com  (905) 648-4797

Funded by the Government of Canada 

# Intention

This collection contains stories, personal essays and futuristic writings. They illuminate facets of humanity that are both wholesome and deadly. There is a subtle tapestry from Indigenous Wisdom throughout the three phases that must apply to our damaged planet if homo-sapiens is to have a home.

PAST dwells on the significance of indigenous history and beliefs, a spirituality that crosses centuries to realize redemption and connection. These stories stand in contrast to the ethnocentric illusions of the wider society where violence, fear and betrayal are rampant. PRESENT includes flash fictions to highlight the destructive illusions *and* the gentle memories of modern society.

The remaining chapters seek to mentor and inspire children to save the world. "Respecting Indigenous Wisdom" provides a pause through poetry to outline a different foundation for humanity. FUTURE is not kind to homo-sapiens and their habitation of Mother Earth. Scientists scramble to provide an exit from the Earth, seeding far away planets. A single person remains in the High Arctic's last outpost while pioneers who occupy a new planet must fight to prevent terrorists from taking it over. Very little has changed.

*Humanity owes an apology to the children of the world.*

# TESTIMONIALS

**Gayle Crosmaz - White Raven**, Spiritual Activator:

I was deeply struck by the poem-chapter *"Respecting Indigenous Wisdom."* It transports one to the river of life, the river of our spirit. The descriptive words capture the imagination as you feel the forest and the rivers rhythm. They remind me of a Wampum Belt teaching I heard at an Elders Gathering. In the final section where Ian talks about *"The Last Man on the Planet"* - Failsafe is the word that jumps off the page for me, as I feel we are currently in that stage by way of nature itself. These are two stand-out chapters in a brilliant array of other chapters.

**Krystina McGuire-Eggins**, Therapist:

Ian Prattis' new book, *"PAST, PRESENT, FUTURE: Stories that Haunt"* is a brilliant collection of stories, writings and essays in fiction and non-fiction. The book leads the reader through thought provoking perspectives about the treatment and respect Western society has thus far shown toward Mother Earth. Dr. Prattis presents the current state of our Earth through a lens that is alarming and sobering at moments. In his true fashion, he offers hope by educating the reader on how Indigenous wisdom that has been passed down for generations can provide a pathway that the human race can choose to embrace for a better future. This is an excellent read, very appropriate for our current times.

**Claudiu Murgan,** Author:

The Spirituality of the indigenous cultures is something that recently, I took a great interest in. It's a facet of humanity that slowly disappears, trampled by the modern mind, too busy with the tangible reality of the surrounding world. Dr. Ian Prattis's *PAST, PRESENT, FUTURE*, tells us to cherish such treasures otherwise we are only empty shells without the meaning and the connection to the spiritual world.

**Jana Begovic**, Novelist, Poet and Senior Editor at *Ariel Chart Literary Journal*:

Prattis' new book, *PAST, PRESENT, FUTURE* is a natural continuation of his long-standing work as an environmental champion. His personal stance toward our planet is that of its custodian and protector. The short fiction and poems in PAST and PRESENT transport the reader to starkly contrasted worlds. The world where indigenous people treaded gently brims with reverence, interconnectedness and sacredness. Prattis immortalizes that sacred relationship between nature and humans. The Chapters in FUTURE offer a glimpse into a disturbing dystopian time that humans created through their insatiable avarice, greed, callousness and neglect. Billions of us may perish under the intolerable climate conditions and pandemics. Have we already passed the point of no return, Prattis asks? At the same time, he offers concrete and helpful advice on how to reduce our own negative environmental footprint. Prattis is an indefatigable warrior, who uses his pen as a sword to fight for a better future.

**Bob Allen**, Founder and CEO IDEAS:

These tales operate at three levels. First, the characters are all of "US." Their stories are the One Human Story of struggling to live in this world. Dig deeper, and you'll find the rich metaphor pointing toward truths about the way our species has evolved and why our permanent dominance of the Earth is a fiction that will not stand up to any real scrutiny. At their root, Dr. Ian Prattis has pointed out that "reality" is not action-over-time but it is *simultaneity*. These stories take their place with other great cultural myths as a shaman's call to the central village fire asking us to listen, engage and imagine.

**Dr. George Pollard**, Associate Professor, Carleton University, Ottawa:

Physics evinces an ostensibly permanent universe. Humanity is not so fortunate. The future of our species, Dr. Prattis candidly argues, is likely precarious; brutal, dark and unsure unless we act now, to solve the climate emergency. Dr. Prattis explores an indigenous past which has an obligation to Past, Present and Future. Greed, he states, drives the PRESENT. Corporations, with rights, abandoned social responsibility, which leads to the collapse of society and, perhaps, the end of our species. The future seems dire, but not necessarily.

The darkness of climate and societal collapse can foster a dreadful dissolution of hope. It is possible to step through the darkness. In doing so, we touch a warm, knowing light that spurs us on, says Dr Prattis, to a more responsible, secure world of our design. From his experience, Dr Prattis learned how indigenous wisdom the world over, protects our species from extinction. His underlying message is that an indigenous approach and modern corporate practices can temper each other to make a better world. Obligations and rights are not incompatible. He makes a compelling case for bringing the Past forward to save all species, including humans, well into the future.

**Germaine De Peralta,** Journalist / Reiki Master Teacher:

Dr. Ian Prattis' new book, **Past, Present, Future** is a testament to the sacred interconnectedness and interdependence of humans, our community, nature, the elements and the animal kingdom. It is these relationships that enable us to survive, thrive, heal and grow. Yet there is an underlying message that these very relationships can become fragile and worn, if we become complacent and fail to nourish and tend to them. Portrayed against a rich backdrop of nature and the seasons, Ian Prattis' stories explore themes of purity and darkness, cruelty and compassion, revenge and forgiveness and finally acceptance. One will delight in the authenticity, depth, and sincerity of his characters.

Finally, there is a prevailing theme of survival and love. And as Prattis writes of love, one would wonder if he, in fact, is in search of the perfect love, or does it really exist? Yet love and beauty go hand-in-hand, and Prattis refuses to abandon his eternal quest for beauty in humanity and in nature, despite their challenges. As a feminist, Dr. Prattis continues to portray his deep respect and reverence for the Divine Feminine and her role in keeping society thriving in the present and into future generations.

## Note from the Author:

I wrote this book *PAST, PRESENT, FUTURE* because I had to.

My responsibility of holding the pen was a mere posture to place words in a sequence that would resonate in the reader's mind.

I had a sense of reciprocity about what I felt was necessary to heal the world from climate emergency and pandemic.

The chapters play their part throughout as a sort of call and response meter that leans on kinship and community rather than corporate greed. The chapters become as seeds in the mind of the reader, so my work cannot be buried or lost.

There is a strong emphasis on Indigenous Wisdom that pulls chapters together while displaying how easy it is to fall into destruction.

## TABLE OF CONTENTS

*Past, Present, Future* / Dr. Ian Prattis

# FOREWORD

## by Judith King Matheson, Elder

I will speak from my heart to all those who may read this brilliant book and use it as a wonderful way to restore relationships and conversations in their families.

For myself, as a Holistic Teacher, from my own life experiences and events that have shaped and moulded me to be as an Elder, a Woman that wears many hats.

My Life experiences began from an age when I was blessed to have a Father and Mother at home eating daily meals as a family discussing the events of the day and world. My Dad taught us to read books, get informed and find and speak our truths and perspectives. This ability to be highly articulate is how books like *Past, Present, Future* could be the powerful resource modern parents can use to once again return to the table.

This book, written by Dr. Ian Prattis, brings back sacred conversations and creates strong, caring, respectful relationships. It returns us to once powerful ways of sharing, talking and inspiring each other.

This is the greatest education I received - being blessed to love books. This is a form of truth telling that is highly healing, for it helps us to grow in relationship with our own selves, our own challenges and our own need to learn how to express our voices in a good way!

In 2021 with the challenges our modern day families are facing, we are given a gift by Dr. Ian Prattis in this book. I believe it meets us where we all are uniquely called, not just to survive these difficult times of change but to thrive.

We engage as families where conversations of the heart invite us to read a book like this one. We can all use it as a powerful resource. In so doing may we as a world and as a society return to our roots. May we see in these times of personal and collective pain a transformation of the old ways to new ways and then back once again. May we all in these times of great truth telling, return to a more caring and compassionate way of being beyond TV, internet, technology and so much noise. See that in sitting in a circle together as a family we have the power to be reminded of simpler ways of living.

We as One Universal Human Family all want the same thing - Peace. I feel opportunity in such books as Ian writes for us. To read and share together opens all possibilities for the modern family to create relationship once again and ignite hearts to have authentic, real, genuine and spiritual conversations. I love the premise of Ian's book, for it addresses very clearly for me why poems, poetry and prose coming from depth can open our minds and hearts. We are living in times of great darkness, but in the knowledge and wisdom of ancient ways of living, there is hope. Spirituality will break through in each new day as I meet a sister/brother and share deep authentic conversations. These are challenging times urging humankind to remember who we are beyond all the trauma of pain, loss, and change that is overwhelming in these times. A resource such as *PAST, PRESENT, FUTURE* - a great gift from my friend Dr. Ian Prattis - opens authentic conversations for us all to share our unique perspectives and to grow!

# PAST

# 1: Four Arrows

She rose from the bed with a dark sense of foreboding.

She shared a cave with her husband, set in the high canyon. She dressed slowly, aware of the shamanic energies arising within her. They directed her to the imminent danger He was walking into. He knew that the larger game migrated toward the east during the day, while resting at night in the canyon valleys nearby.

She stood very still at the lip of the cave, observing the first rays of daylight caressing the valley below their cave. She swayed back and forth in the early morning breeze sensing the energies arising within her mind and body. Rooted in one spot, she concentrated on him.

She could foresee the danger. Without waking Elder Sister, She took down her powerful long bow from the cave wall, selecting his four best arrows. She knew she would need every one of them, as she stilled her fear.

He had left carefully so his tracks were scarcely visible.

Drawing on her mountain upbringing – she knew the trace of every creature, She quickly found his footprints, following them eastwards. She noticed a rock cache with small animals that He had hunted, along with several broken arrows. Not the game He was looking for, but vital to keep them alive. She carefully replaced the rocks exactly as they had been built. The tracks led her to a dry gulch where she saw the heavier print of his forward foot. Again, She sensed the shamanic energies. This was where He had stood to shoot a larger game animal from his bow.

He had stood in that exact spot at dawn, drawing a steady bead on a large mule deer with his last arrow. His previous arrows had shattered on impact but his final arrow was made from stronger wood and would deeply penetrate the unaware mule deer, starkly outlined by the early morning sun.

As He released the arrow from his bow, the prey moved in the same instant. The strong, swift arrow did not provide a clean kill. It went deeply into the mule deer, high in the muscles of the left foreleg, missing the heart and cutting through sinews and muscles. He whispered a prayer to the animal for causing unnecessary suffering.

He proceeded to follow the wounded creature to end its misery. The erratic and painful trail left by the dying mule deer strayed into Tonto Apache territory.

He caught up with the mule deer, exhausted and on its knees, close to a sandstone butte reaching into the morning sky. He dispatched it with his hunting knife and enacted his gratitude by cutting out part of the heart and liver, placing them on a natural rock altar. He put tobacco by the stone as an offering.

As He began to gut and skin the mule deer, He became acutely aware that He was no longer alone.

Scanning his surrounding, he noted three Apache warriors. One of them, the smallest, was scaling the sandstone butte to gain an advantage. The other two approached in a pincer movement that provided no escape. He knew they could kill him. He had only his hunting knife and a bow without arrows. As He slowly backed into the rock face of the sandstone butte, a spontaneous, silent shout screamed in his mind calling out to her for help.

And there She was. Standing with her bow fully drawn, She commanded the edge of a clearing close to the sandstone butte, well shielded from sight by small ash trees.

Her first arrow sent death screeching to the warrior climbing the butte piercing him through the heart, He fell with a heavy thud on the rocky floor below.

Her surprise attack prompted the tallest warrior to run towards her at the edge of the clearing though an arrow was already coming his way from her bow. It went right through his neck. As he turned, dropping his weapons while clutching at his throat, her third arrow found his heart killing him instantly.

The third warrior was in fierce hand-to-hand battle with her husband and had gained the upper hand, throwing him against the rock wall of the red sandstone butte. As the Apache raised his battle axe to strike a death blow, her fourth arrow, shot powerfully with great accuracy, entered below his armpit and ripped through his chest into the heart. The warrior fell forward.

Her husband tore the battleaxe from his assailant and finished the death process with a swift smash to the skull. It was over in a matter of seconds. Breathing heavily, He stood there with the warrior's battleaxe in his hand.

She, with the stealth of a mountain lion, approached the two other warriors, now motionless on the ground. Her hunting knife was drawn, but there was no need. They were both dead.

She walked slowly towards him. He was in total awe of this magnificent woman, his wife. He fell to his knees in front of her and wept as He wrapped his strong arms around her legs. She pulled him to his feet and gently wiped his tears away.

His voice came out as a sob. "Did you hear me…?

"My husband, I heard your shouted scream long before you uttered it in your mind. I knew what was to happen and have been tracking you since dawn."

He could never understand her gifts of seeing and felt humbled by her presence in his life. She was filled with gratitude that his life was still with her, as she feared the dislocation a different outcome would have created. They stood together, motionless for a moment, then his strategic sense asserted itself.

"We must take the arrows out of the slain Apaches and from the mule deer so we are not identified. Leave the bodies right here, just where they have fallen. The animals and vultures will come and scatter their remains and cover some of our tracks."

She nodded her consent. The sun had begun to rise and they had to be meticulous. They created a false trail to a pass in the canyon wall that lead to the southern plateaus. Retracing their steps to the killing ground by the sandstone butte, they began the slow removal of all traces of their passage westwards.

He took care to relocate the rock cache he had built for the small animals he had killed - two rabbits and several small grouse. He retrieved his shattered arrows and threw the rocks into the pinyon pine forest, leaving one dead grouse for vultures to find and scatter their unmistakable presence over their tracks.

As night fell, they rested under a large rocky outcrop sheltered from view by a clump of juniper trees. Safe from any scouting party, it had a clear vista of the steep path that led to this temporary sanctuary. The night was warm, and they listened carefully for sounds of movement but did not detect any sign of an Apache pursuit.

A curious desert badger inspected them, grunting and growling. They saw the outlines of mule deer in the valley below, and they listened to the evening chorus of insects and lizards. The deep coughing sound of a cougar caused him to stiffen and regret He had no arrows. He looked around for rocks that would fit into his fist and glanced up at the evening light. A golden eagle had settled in the high branches of a tall pine. He relaxed, suddenly feeling safe with this night companion confirming affinity since his childhood.

Before the break of dawn they continued their careful journey, with many detours to throw off any pursuers, before they got close to the safe haven of their cave.

She stopped and gave the woman's small grouse call.

Elder Sister loomed out of the morning darkness with her long bow leveled at them and her battle axe slung over one shoulder. She had stationed herself at a hidden juncture of the trail leading to their cave, ready for the worst. Elder Sister had sensed the same foreboding that drew Younger Sister out at dawn, but did not have her gifts of seeing.

He whispered briefly about what had happened. Elder Sister nodded silently and beckoned them to go on to the cave while she checked that they had not been followed. She returned several hours later in the dark.

They did not light a fire, instead wrapping themselves in blankets and animal skins for warmth. They humbly offered prayers for the three slain Apache warriors. They did not leave the cave for a week, surviving on dried berries, water and their scant supply of dried meat. Elder Sister maintained a sharp vigilance during this time, her long bow trained on the trail far below.

No-one came their way. They were safe.

*Past, Present, Future* / Dr. Ian Prattis

# 2: Love Lost and Dark Shadows

Andrew and Lorna left the dance and walked to the hill, looking at the moon hovering over the sea.

Andrew's jacket was about Lorna's shoulders as the ocean and land exchanged their silences. The young couple had known each other since childhood, inevitably drawn together in an often volatile attraction.

Their easy childhood friendship grew stronger through grade school and high school, but now, as young adults they entered a clumsy courtship.

Though they loved each other, their relationship had severe ups and downs. During a past fierce argument Lorna slapped his face and Andrew retaliated. But he knew he was much stronger and he begged her to forgive him. She did but spoke firmly, "I will forgive you this once, but do not ever lift your hand to hit me again."

That evening this past violence was not a part of their coming together. He kissed her gently and his lips burned at the touch of her. There was a tumult in his chest as her beauty and independence drew him to her. The demands of their waking hearts and strong young limbs could not be denied. They made love to one another, sweetly and tenderly. The heather pillowed their beauty as they reached up to the universe of stars that threw a dreamlike blanket over them.

Andrew looked at the delicate and beautiful face cradled in his arms and picked a buttercup and placed it on her lips, and kissed the flower. He kissed her cheek and teased her gently. "Will you be my flower now Lorna?"

"You must say that to every girl you take to the heather," she retorted.

There was more than teasing in her reply. There was a deep wistfulness. Her heart welled with love for him, but sensed that he had this for everyone. She wanted to be more to him than just everyone. He chuckled at her reply for he knew it was wrong, though it was believed of him.

They lay side by side in the heather on that warm summer's night cradled by the moon's glow. Andrew talked of the stars and the sea and of how one day he would write of the things he felt and opened himself to Lorna. She had never seen this depth in him and was afraid that she could not follow him. His voice softly caressed her and she regained her strength and love as she listened.

They were constantly with one another after that. His mother, Annie, was pleased as she scented marriage between them, but Andrew had no thoughts for settling down. He simply delighted in being fully with Lorna, yet the small spark that she had lit in him grew faster than his mind allowed.

Two months later she was not there to meet his fishing boat when he docked at the pier. Andrew could not wait to see her, but had to remain aboard until every task had been completed. Such was his way.

As soon as he was ready, Andrew quickly strode to her house and was told she had taken a walk to the hills.

He followed the directions given and he trod the path that led him to where they had first made love. He found her sitting there looking out to sea. She was very quiet, pale and ill. He saw this and approached her quickly and sat beside her.

"What is it Lorna that makes you so pale?"

She did not answer him so that he had to move in front of her to face her. There was such concern and tenderness in his voice. He saw the tears in her eyes and softly insisted that she speak to him.

"I'm having a baby Andrew. I'm two months pregnant by you." They had only made love that one time, here in this place.

"Is that why you came here?" he asked.

She nodded through her tears. He reached out to her and gently touched her cheek with his fingers so that she would look at him. When she did he smiled.

"We'll be wed Lorna and I'll be lucky to have you as a wife."

She moved away from his touch and shouted at him, "Just like that? We'll be wed. Not I love you Lorna. Not will you marry me Lorna. Just we'll be wed because you've made me pregnant. You'd wed any girl you impregnated. I'm no different am I?" she asked desperately, for her heart was breaking as she spoke these words to him.

Andrew was taken aback and stumbled clumsily over his words, but she rebuffed him.

"Please listen to me Lorna, my words are all wrong but can you not see what's in my eyes and in my heart. I want you for my own. The baby is just bringing it about faster than I thought. I want you as my wife. I've not known how to ask you." He said at last.

Lorna could not see and answered Andrew's endearments with her own pain and bitter views. "Don't tell me that, for it's not so," she cried out. "You don't understand yourself. You love everyone. You would marry fat Jessie with the warts and be content. I-I must have more than that for I love you completely, whereas you cannot love me more than anyone else. It's not kindness I want, it's your love - all of it. I'll not be like other women and accept less or tie a man with a child and be happy with a small piece of his affection. I want more than you are prepared to give."

Andrew implored her to believe him that she had lit a spark that coursed and burned through all of him. But Lorna believed him not. She left him there, puzzled and bewildered. He was hurt and confused and knew not what to do. So he left her to herself.

Lorna waited for him. For two days she waited for him in quiet desperation and panic, and when he did not come she took herself to Glasgow.

She was gone several weeks, a time that Andrew passed in utmost misery. This was all beyond his understanding.

Lorna returned pale and brittle and he went to her and they walked to their place in the heather for they knew not how to talk to one another. Andrew could not stand it. With a cry he held her and begged her to give him her love, he could not bear her to be distant from him.

Her hands trembled as he touched her. His heart drained at the sadness in her large blue eyes as he stood before her.

"I've had an abortion Andrew."

Time stopped. The rocks and earth absorbed her words. Andrew scarcely heard. He stood stupidly looking at her, not seeing or hearing but frozen and rooted like a dead tree.

"An abortion. In Glasgow," Lorna whispered this quietly.

His hand, driven by his seaman's strength, moved through the air and he hit her and felled her. He recoiled and then looked in horror at the hand that had struck his Lorna.

"Oh God forgive me. Jesus save me," he cried as he moved to pick her up. "Forgive me Lorna, please forgive me. My hand had a mind of its own. Lorna wait for me."

There was blood on her lips and teeth as she quickly backed away from him. She was like a wounded tigress and had no mercy or forgiveness.

"Lorna for God's sake what is happening to us? I want to be your husband and enjoy our bairns. What in Jesus's name have you done? Why have you done this to me?"

"To you?!?" Lorna cried, incredulous and brave. She stepped towards him. The bruise from his hand had reddened her face from chin to eyebrow. "To you! Nothing has been done to you. I did it to me, Andrew, not to you and I'll carry the sin of it to my grave."

Andrew stumbled back at her fierceness.

"I did it to me, do you hear! I also told you years ago never to raise your hand to me again and what did you just do to me?" she shouted and the breeze took her words and the sea received them.

"This abortion - I did it to me!" she shouted.

They faced one another with tragic intensity.

"Why Lorna, tell me why?" There were tears running down his face.

"You ask me why. It's so I'm free of marrying you, so that you are free of marrying me because I'm with child. Also, I do not want to get hurt by your strong hands. We're not meant for one another and a child would have bound us."

Andrew fell to his knees on the ground before her. His tears turned to a strangled sob. He cried as though his guts would come through his mouth. He cried in this terrible fashion and collapsed prostrate on the ground with his face in the soft earth. His hands reached out and he held her foot with one hand and ground the hand that hit her into the earth to cleanse his brutality. She flinched at his touch but watched his demented torment as he wept.

It was just as her own when she had stumbled away from the abortionist's house - a tired Glasgow doctor who spared her from the horrors of the back streets. Andrew wept as something precious and rare had gone from him and he did not know what to do.

Lorna raised him and they stood together, terrible in their shared pain. Soon Andrew was silent. He sat and rested his head on the heather. He was stunned and ashamed but could think of nothing but Lorna and her pain. He spoke to her, words of life and love. He tried to lift her burden to his own shoulders so that she may have peace. He felt her desperation and pain and asked her to accept him, pledging his life and strength to her if she would take him. He stood and begged forgiveness and sought her love.

She shook her head slowly, her eyes full of sadness and pain.

"There can be no going back, Andrew. This will always lie between us."

He protested that this was not so, that they needed each other to heal and grow, but already his hold on Lorna was slipping away.

Her heart already broken she whispered "It's no use," with a finality that he should have fought. They were both terribly harmed and could not find a way to bridge the abyss they had opened. As proud young persons they did not even seek help from those close to them – Annie, his mother, with her intuition and her uncle Colin with his worldly wisdom. And so they forgot their beauty and hurled themselves into a hell that scarred them deeply for life.

There were times Andrew's soul talked to him, to go to her wherever she was. She had been deeply hurt as he had been hurt and she needed him as he needed her. But so convinced was he of her hate that he let her go and he bore within himself the guilt of what he had done. It was to free him she said, so his was the pain and the guilt and the deep, enduring sorrow. And for the second time he did not go to her, but she was never from his mind and heart. His loss became a memory that turned into a scar that would not heal.

He returned to the sea and despised himself. His dark shadow of self-contempt seeped into his relations with other men.

On board the boats, he drove the crew to the very limits of their endurance and they learned to fear rather than love him. He had no regard for his own safety and little for theirs, yet they remained with him, to protect him. They sensed something terrible had happened which he would not speak of. The harder he became the more successfully did he sweep the sea of its bounty and men followed him now more for wealth and not for respect.

There were whispers that he would go the way of his father's madness, so grim and distant did he become. He bled for Lorna and when no-one saw he cried for her and lost her, for he did not understand what he could have done.

He never ever forgave himself for striking her with his hand. His mother Annie gave him comfort as she had as a child, not understanding his pain but for once leaving her tongue still.

Had she known the cause she would have taken him to Lorna herself. She would have understood as only a woman could - the need and love that the girl's bitterness shielded. But she never knew and stilled her tongue when it should have probed and demanded knowledge. He lived thus, only half a man, crushing the sensitivity in his soul and driving all but his mother away from him. He could not let them see into the dark window of his soul, so deeply did he suffer.

His mother worried at his state. She was frail now and failing but her son saw nothing of this, so enmeshed was he in his self-disgust. She would walk to the point by the bay to look for his boat passing through the sound even when she knew he was not to be expected. She walked in memory of her late husband Brendan, who had died suddenly after coming down with catatonic mental illness. She preferred calling to mind where they had kissed when young and longed to be united with him again.

Only her frail flesh prevented her final journey and oft times she was impatient that she should still live. Just as quickly she would brush away her blasphemy and thank her God for life. She mused on these thoughts as she rested at the point, looking to the sea. She was startled to see Andrew's boat approaching the sound and hastily rose to return home to prepare a dinner for him.

She turned to hurry along the path. A swift immense stroke came over her and she slowly crumpled to the ground. She slowly regained consciousness and struggled to her feet, cursing her fainting, barely noticing that her left arm and leg moved only with great difficulty. She sensed her late husband close by and thought little of her painful progression along the path.

As she opened the garden gate a final, massive stroke hit her overburdened heart and the sky revolved about her and with relief she sank to the earth and met her Brendan.

Andrew's boat passed through the sound and made for the fishing grounds to the south-west. He was there for two days and returned to dock on the third day.

He left his crew to take the catch to market and walked home. He entered the house and called to his mother. There was no answer.

He crossed to the back door and stepped into the garden. Then he saw her huddled by the gate. Though rigor mortis had set in, Annie was leaning against the gate with a faint smile on her face as she reunited with her late husband.

Andrew picked her up and blindly carried her into the house, setting her gently upon her bed. He tried to straighten her limbs but could not. He had no heart to cry or weep or think. He stood in her bedroom with his head bowed and the breath came thickly and heavily from his chest.

"Why?"

The small thought was released to his mind and built up in his head, growing larger and louder until it exploded from his lips.

"Why?"

His hands gripped the back of the chair he was leaning on as he bellowed in rage, voice to his wrath, pain and sorrow.

"Why?"

He picked up the chair and hurled it through the window. The shattering of the glass drew him to more destruction. The only act of being he now possessed was to destroy and he bellowed and roared through the house, smashing and breaking with his great strength. His mother lay dead and at peace while he destroyed whatever was about him.

Old Colin – Lorna's uncle - ill in bed, heard him from his own farm house and stumbled up the track to Andrew's house. He heard the bellows and roars of an animal in fury and could scarce believe it was Andrew.

Colin entered the house and saw the devastation. Standing in the midst of it was his young friend, whose wild eyes caught the old man and it was almost with a triumph that he pointed to his mother's room. Colin entered and his heart filled with grief to see Annie so. He also saw the look of peace on her face, and briefly knelt to pray for her soul.

"Why, Colin?"

It was an urgent desperate whisper from Andrew. At Colin's silence the storm of wrath swept his voice to a roar. "Is there a curse on our family?" He shouted at the old man. "What have we done to deserve this? My father mad, now this, my mother."

Colin started to speak, to calm him, but the anger and grief were too strong.

"Everyone I touch suffers, even your niece Lorna."

Colin looked sharply at him, but Andrew could not go on. He was finished at the mention of Lorna's name and Colin led him away and called for others to see to Annie and to the destruction in the house.

Colin tried to reach the young man he loved but there were barriers, grief and torment that he could not cross.

Andrew stumbled away from him, from his house and drowned himself in the oblivion that drink is kind enough to give. In whisky and gin and finally in anything that had a taste of alcohol, he found a place to keep himself away from pain.

Andrew drank while he was awake and slept wherever he fell - in ditches, on doorsteps, on kitchen floors. His kinsfolk and friends tried to reach him, to bring him back. Oh, how they tried. But he had locked himself from them and answered their kindness with abuse and drunkenness.

 His boat lay at the dock for fully a month until the mate went out with it. Still his folk gave only kindness, and it was kindness that eventually left him alone, to wander and shuffle about the island from farm to pub, pub to dock, pier to pub, in a constant never ending oblivion of drink and delirium.

The source of the pain and agony of losing the love of Lorna was long forgotten, as he relentlessly drowned his will. The islanders bore his pain with him, caring for him, but he would not let their love come to him. In his mind he had failed everyone.

The animals at Andrew's farm were the only creatures that kept him this side of sanity as he tended to their needs. In rare moments of sobriety he fished for himself, setting lines and traps for lobsters, crabs and cod in the sea near his house. It was pathetic that he, the best fisherman in the islands, should cast a line from a small dinghy. But he did it and took some solace in his return to a primitive survival. He set the lines further out to sea and rowed his dinghy once a week to lift the sea's gift.

Andrew's judgment and seamanship had become careless, almost as if he willingly dropped his guard for the sea to deliver the blow he longed for. He took no notice of the dark streaked clouds that reared suddenly in the sky. He took his oars and rowed out to sea.

The clouds darkened as the rapidly advancing cold air lifted the warm front that hung over the sea. It tossed violently into the sky, creating sudden and vicious turbulence.

Andrew did not notice the gathering storm, until he felt the dinghy being moved and driven by power not from his arms. The fierce wind had caught the tail of the ebb tide and they ran in opposed directions with the small dinghy caught between them.

The swell of the sea that had been hardly visible now rose in menacing ridges of water that raced straight for the boat. Andrew turned the prow of the boat into the huge swell. As he fought to keep the boat into the swell, one of his oars snapped in two.

He slowly straightened with the broken oar in his hand and he saw in the sea his chance to end it all.

"Take me," he bellowed. "Finish it."

The boat turned sluggishly and was hit beam on by the next wave and spun into the trough, keeling dangerously to one side but it righted itself and rolled over the top of the swell. He was standing, waiting. The boat turned too slowly for the next wave that towered above it. Andrew welcomed it, as a huge hammer blow split the boat's keel from its beam.

As the boat rose in the air with its back broken, he was hurled into the sea. Gratefully he went down and did not struggle against the cold grip the sea had on him. He came to the surface and felt nothing.

Andrew wondered if he was already dead. The current that ran there swept him towards tidal reefs, battering his body on the outcrops of rock and leaving him atop a slime-covered skerry.

The sea continued to crash over him, but with less intensity as the tide fell. He was alive. The sea would not take him.

He waited for the tide to turn again and before it could advance he clambered over the rocks and swam to the shore. He dragged himself painfully to his house, delirious and incoherent and would let no man help him until he had drunk himself into a stupor. Once drunk he knew they could not help him.

He continued his course of self-destruction for many years until folk learned to ignore him, and forgot what he once was and could have been. He saw himself one night in the bar of the pub, glancing at the mirror. His mind floated free from his body and rested to look at himself. He saw a terrible, ragged, pathetic creature stumbling from table to table slobbering stupidly, begging for a drink. His mind took this in but slowly. *That's not me. It cannot be me.* The mind gasped.

*It's not me. It cannot be myself over there.* The mind looked, noticing the expressions of pity and disgust on the faces of men that knew him. He saw himself fall over a table and bring the glasses of beer and whisky spilling into the laps of the men drinking there. With a curse an Aberdeen fisherman with beer splashed over him took Andrew by the shoulders and shook him and ordered him away. The mind saw its body and face stand there stupidly grinning at the east coast man still begging for a drink.

Andrew did not feel the punch that split his nose and sent him crashing into another table. His body rolled over and he got to its feet, still grinning stupidly as the blood ran from its face.

Four strong island men moved towards his tormentor and threw the man from Aberdeen out of that place. They were ashamed of Andrew but he was their own. In their pity and disgust they protected him and took the wreck of a man home, leaving Andrew at the door of his house.

With sadness and loathing they walked away. The mind called to them his gratitude and new knowledge, as the mouth on it slobbered and grinned stiffly through caked blood and alcohol.

The different parts of his soul were left to battle one with the other. There was nothing that man and conscience could do. So he was left there, seeing himself anew... In the very depths of hell he was left there.

# 3: Homecoming – Part One

Steven Martin was a retired mariner, known throughout the islands for his kindness and wisdom. Yet in his later years he would isolate himself for reasons only he knew.

One evening in the 'midst of a summer storm his isolation was suddenly usurped. There was a loud knock on the door of his house. Steven was dosing in the shabby armchair by his fire. He half-awoke listening to the gale that had come surprisingly. His eyes closed again. The knock was louder and more insistent. He stepped to the door and unbolted it. There was a man at his step, soaked to the skin and wild-eyed.

"Can you give us shelter?" the man cried.

Steven looked at him without seeing, his mind far away with other thoughts.

"We're camping a little way from here and the storm has ripped our tents. Will you give us shelter? Your house is the only light for miles." The young man stood shivering in the doorway, unsure of whether the gaunt man facing him understood a word.

"There's room in the barn behind you there." Steven's voice sounded thin and distant, as he directed the young man to where his animals were kept. The man looked steadily at him for a moment, thanked him then was gone.

Steven closed the door and went to sit by his fire, drifting back towards where he had left his thoughts. He hummed softly to himself, listened to the winds and started to fall asleep. Then suddenly he stood up with a jerk as though stung. He remembered the two tents pitched near his farm. There was a woman and child with the man. He had noticed them and avoided them, though he had admired the site they had chosen. It was close to water and sheltered from the wind's intentions.

"My God," he whispered to himself, "what have I become. Lord, forgive a stupid old man - Jesus save me," he muttered. "God forgive me for turning a stranger away."

He plunged out of the house into the storm and picked his way in the dark to the barn. When he opened the door the young man was spreading a sodden sleeping bag on the hay, trying to comfort his sobbing wife The child, a girl, sat amidst the hay, her great round eyes unaccustomed to the turmoil and tears. A lantern swinging from a beam cast its light back and forth infesting the barn with changing patterns of shadows. The child cried out in terror as Steven stood in the doorway. The lantern illuminated his gauntness. He appeared a terrible figure with the wind in his hair and a stick in his hand.

Steven stood motionless. His mouth worked but words would not come. The struggle for speech contorted his features, and the child shrank behind her mother for protection. Help me damn you, pleaded Steven in his speechless void. Time seemed to suspend itself as the four remained frozen in amazement and fear. Then Steven found words to suit his tongue. He said softly:

"Would you please come to my house?"

The quietness and humility of his voice enabled them to relax. The family breathed but did not move. Without a word Steven gathered an armful of their belongings and reached out to take the child by the hand. She shrank away from him.

"Bring your daughter to the warmth, there's a fire at my house." They entered his home and sat awkwardly. Steven built up the fire to make them warm and dry.

As Steven bustled about in the kitchen making tea and bannocks he caught a glimpse of himself in the window. He had rough stubble at his chin and his hair stood stiff from the wind. Carrying the tea tray into the living room, he turned with a gentle laugh to the child, "No wonder you were frightened lassie. I look like the devil himself." He set down the tray and combed his hair with his fingers. "Is that better? No?"

She stared at him with large eyes, still afraid.

"I will shave this off then." He said to her as he pointed to the stubble on his chin. He took some hot water from the kettle and set a bowl and small cracked mirror on a chair. He fetched his shaving brush and a bar of soap. He sat before the mirror and slowly worked a lather with the brush and shaved his whiskers off with a razor.

"Now that is much better don't you think?"

She giggled.

His eyes caught those of her father and in a moment of silence begged forgiveness. The young man smiled and nodded. Steven asked the girl if she liked music. She smiled as Steven brought out an old accordion. His clumsy fingers coaxed music from it and the child laughed and clapped her hands. She sat near him and he played for her, and felt pulsing through him the chords of life he had almost forgotten. He nodded in time to his music. There was a sweet tiredness that everyone felt. The storm continued outside. He brought his music to an end, and they sat in a pleasurable silence.

"And your name sir?" It was the young man asking.

"It is Steven. Big Steven Martin," he smiled wryly. "But I've become awful shrunken of late." The evening took away his caution and he hid nothing from them. It was only he who did not see that his beauty was beginning to reflect in their eyes.

"I'm Mathew," the young man said, "and this is my wife Johanna and my daughter Helen."

"Helen is it?" The child nodded. "I once knew a Helen, but I lost her long ago." He mused absently to himself.

Helen came to him and shyly placed her small hand on his, and he took her in his arms and held her for a moment. "That's a great gift you hand to me," he said at last. Her parents did not understand his sentiment. They only saw a gentleness and tenderness that deeply moved them. Their daughter, a child of seven, soon slept beside Steven on the couch. Each one there in that comfortable quiet, instinctively knew that they were to be caught up in the web of the others' lives.

"There's a bed that's been warming in the back room for you mistress."

Johanna got up and took her sleeping daughter from him and smiled gratefully.

"Your man can take this day bed here," he said.

"And where will you sleep?" she asked.

A look of mischief twinkled in his eyes. "The barn will be my bed tonight, mistress."

Mathew protested and said, "No Steven, you cannot do that just because we are here."

Then he saw the humour in Steven's eyes and laughed softly with him.

Steven chuckled "Don't worry about that. There's many a night I've been more comfortable there than here, maybe not tonight though!"

Johanna took Helen to bed and the two men talked by the fire, at ease and comfortable with one another. They hid nothing, as strangers will sometimes do when they meet. Mathew was an author, a successful playwright and they talked of books and literature. He was amazed at Steven's literary knowledge and basked in his perception and sensitivity.

"You should have been a writer, Steven."

"Perhaps I should have. Life just took me on a different path." Steven paused for a long while. "It was a path of sorrow that was too much for me. I allowed myself to become separate from the world of humanity. I lost my "song." When I retired from the Merchant Navy it felt as though my life was somehow over and had no purpose." He looked into the fire. "There once was a chance to be a writer, but I could not take it." There was no bitterness or regret in the telling.

"Could you not write, yet?" Mathew asked.

Steven shook his head slowly. "No, I think not. My song was near finished, though your daughter Helen may well have brought it back to life." He chuckled at that insight, startled that he would reveal so much to a stranger. He looked up and saw the dawn's first light showing its way through the window. "Look, the pair of us have talked the night away. You must sleep now."

*****

Johanna found them asleep, Mathew in the chair, Steven upon the day bed. She looked around at the walls and the heavy solid furniture, frayed and dirty, yet she warmed to it. She went into the kitchen and explored the scullery and made tea and breakfast for the sleeping men. Her daughter was shushed quiet so that they may sleep. The smell of eggs, toast and ham brought Mathew and Steven from the depths of their slumber. When Steven awoke and opened his eyes, Helen was there holding a mug of tea for him. He smiled slowly and took the cup from her. She returned with his breakfast. He thanked her with a grave courtesy, which she answered with a hesitant smile, then raced back to the kitchen to her mother.

He felt a warmth, as he slowly ate his breakfast. He then thanked his Lord for the brief gift of this family. Though Mathew had finished his breakfast he enjoyed the morning's silence with him. Their eyes met, and held, then moved on. There was to be nothing taken back. They had started with openness and confidence and nothing of their long talking was to be excised. The morning was grey and dull but did not deter Mathew from accepting Steven's invitation to walk to the shore. Johanna and Helen remained behind. The two men resumed their talking and further explored one another's thoughts and feelings. Steven delighted Mathew with the sandy bay cradled between the two ridges of his farm. He pointed out the different flowers and birds. As luck would have it, they also saw a family of otters by the stream leading into the bay. It was exhilarating for both men to listen to one another. It was the middle of the afternoon before they returned.

Steven entered his house by the front door and stepped towards the fire in the main room. He stopped and slowly looked around him. Everything was in its place just as before, but it had been transformed. His heavy and dull furniture gleamed with polish. The whitewashed walls had been scrubbed and light poured in through the newly cleaned windows. The curtains had been thrown back to let in the day and his day bed was covered with a large check blanket. Flowers were placed in jars by the fire and windows and above the fireplace.

"You did this?" he asked of Johanna and Helen. "Why, it's beautiful. Who would believe it?" He turned and looked at Helen, "You did this?" Helen nodded, excited that he seemed so pleased. He walked around in wonder at the simple beauty they had added. "Thank you both. You're bringing an old man to life."

It was Mathew who broke the spell. "It's time we were on our way, Johanna. I'll help you pack."

He put his hand out to Steven. "I'm grateful for your help Steven and your friendship. We must go to the village and see about a place to stay for the rest of our holiday." There was an uncomfortable silence as they stood, waiting.

"You're going from here?" asked Steven incredulously. "Will you not stay?" He looked to Mathew, then Johanna and finally to Helen, "My house is yours for as long as you may wish."

Mathew shifted nervously "That's very kind of you but we can't impose ourselves on you, intrude on your peace and solitude. We'll find a place in the village."

"Intrude, impose, what are you talking of Mathew?" Steven spoke quickly "I've been silent and isolated for too long. I want you to stay. This is for me as much as for you." There was a moment of unease between them as Mathew stood, unable to express how he dreaded walking away from Steven, his house and the depth of new friendship he had glimpsed.

Johanna stepped to Steven and put her arm in his. "We would love to stay, Steven." She rested her head on his shoulder.

So they stayed, prolonging their holiday for an extra month. Steven had never felt so happy in his life. They walked together, told stories and were silent when it rained. He opened the wonders of the island to them. He and the child spent hours and days in one another's company, crossing the hills to the Atlantic. Helen filled with excitement, not knowing that she and her parents brought him back from his retreat into self-destruction. People saw and whispered and pointed. Some were happy for him, some felt envious that it should be strangers that he welcomed, while others cared not at all. All too soon it was over. Mathew, Johanna and Helen left for their home in Cumberland where Mathew worked at his writing and Johanna taught music. It had been a wonderful awakening for Steven.

In the months after they left he recalled to his mind every incident of his knowing of them. He thought of them as he retraced the walks they took in concert, remembering the awe of the child at seeing eagles fly and gannets plunge into the sea. He was grateful to them.

*****

The young family came the next summer to stay with him. Days of sunshine and grace warmed their hearts and bodies. Dawn came early with sun filtered dew and breezes from the sea gently sweeping the shore and hills. Each day was a drawn-out spectrum of life, rich with colour.

They enjoyed that there was light until nearly midnight and they could sleep then, eager and expectant of the morning to come. Children grew brown as they swam in the bays and scrambled on the hills. Men and women were in the hay fields with scythes. Slowly and rhythmically cutting acres of tall lush grass to bring in as winter-feed for their animals. The smell of the hay and the flowers was a perfume they inhaled. Crops of potatoes and vegetables in the raised beds were weeded and tended and grew strong in the heat and gentle rain that came, enough to nurture their growing.

Steven's heart was full. He was restored to his own people and the young family had found a place to live a scarce four miles from him. The schoolhouse at the head of the next bay. It was a fine building, set into the hill beside the river that rushed to the sea loch that stretched before it. Steven was constantly with them and enjoyed their life and vitality. But a worry lay in his mind when they talked of how they would transform the schoolhouse into a new home for themselves. The child, Helen, had already planned that Steven would live with them when he became old. He chuckled at her warmth and love, though sensed it would not happen at that place. The friendship between the two men deepened. Mathew felt the added wisdom and gentleness in the old man. His work became dusted with Steven's dignity and began to show a maturity and breadth of vision not there in his previous writings. The two were locked in thought and word. Johanna and Helen were part of it all. Their summer continued in this way, a rare idyll of peace and harmony.

Johanna was having lunch with Steven at the schoolhouse. She mentioned to him that Mathew was going to buy the schoolhouse. She said, "The sea and hills are an inspiration for Mathew's writing – and we can be near to you."

A frown passed over Steven's face. "Is there something wrong, Steven?" Johanna asked.

"There may well be," he turned thoughts in his mind. "John Menzie who owns the schoolhouse, is not honest. I would not trust him. Tell me how far you have gone with this?"

She replied, "Mathew has agreed to a purchase this coming July and Mr. Menzie agreed to let us occupy the place this June for our summer holiday. He seems very generous and obliging."

It worried Steven and nagged at his mind – this business. Mathew walked into the kitchen.

"I see Joanna's let my secret out. You don't like Menzie"

"It's not a matter of dislike, only distrust. What have you agreed to?"

Mathew outlined his meetings with Menzie in Glasgow, to arrive at their final agreement on a price.

Steven shook his head slowly, puzzled by something in Mathew's tone. "There's more to it than this, is there not?"

Mathew answered hesitatingly. "Yes, there is. Part of our agreement is that I pay half the price direct to him and it's the remaining half that is declared as the buying price. It saves him from paying an awful lot in taxes."

"How much money does he want?" queried Steven.

"Well there's five thousand pounds that will go to him and the same amount through his solicitor. I don't object to anyone dodging the taxman, Steven, the government gets enough out of us."

Steven sucked on his teeth and exhaled slowly. "That's of no account. I've been doing the same for years with one thing or another. But I don't feel right about this deal you have with Menzie."

"What is there to be lost? Menzie makes a pile of money, and gets rid of a place that he doesn't want and we get to live and grow in a home that we've always dreamed of."

"Don't build the dreams yet Mathew," Steven said finally. "I'll say no more but mark your step with Menzie." He abruptly changed the direction of their talk, when Helen pulled at his hand, as it was time for a walk.

It was late one evening a few weeks later that Mathew and Johanna returned to the schoolhouse from a hike along the loch. They could not believe their good fortune that they were to own this place. They were quiet and content with one another. Helen was playing in her new bedroom upstairs. As they looked from their front window over the loch they saw a large van draw up to their door. John Menzie and four other men got out.

"What can they be wanting at this time of night?" Johanna asked.

"He's probably after an extra thousand pounds under the table," Mathew replied in jest, but he was frowning as the men came to the door. Menzie walked in without knocking and entered the room where Mathew and Johanna were waiting.

He jerked his thumb to the road. "Out you go." There was an incredulous silence. Neither Mathew or Johanna understood him. Menzie repeated with added emphasis. "*Out you go.* Get your bags packed and out of my house. Me and my men are staying here for the rest of the summer."

Mathew was the first to recover. "What the hell do you mean, bursting in like this?"

Menzie surveyed him very coolly. "I'm telling you to get out of my house. If you're not quick about it - these men will simply throw you out." His four companions, scraped from Glasgow's gutters, stood there, grinning at the couple's discomfort, willing them to resist, to refuse, so they could impose their violence on them.

"But we're on holiday and we're buying this place from you" Johanna cried out.

"Not anymore, you're not," Menzie said harshly. 'The deal's off, I've different plans for this place."

Mathew's anger mounted, "You can't do this. Not in this day and age,"

Menzie laughed at him. "Who will stop me? Show me the lease on this place, your rental agreement with me. Now don't tell me you don't have anything in writing. What a shame."

Mathew clenched his fists as he was visibly shaken. There was no written agreement between them, just a handshake - a mere handshake. He collected himself, pale and icily calm. "Johanna, go to Steven and ask him to come here." As she hesitated he urged her to immediately go.

Menzie added for good measure, "On you go now. Go and see that old bastard, for you'll be staying with him before the night's out. I do not give a damn about him or you"

Johanna left and Mathew, controlling his anger, coldly watched the men come in. Menzie picked up his bag and went to climb the stairs. He found his way barred by Mathew's slight figure.

"You will not go up Menzie, my daughter is playing there."

There was a quiet and dangerous intensity to Mathew. One of the Glasgow toughs advanced threateningly but was waved back.

"You'll be out of here soon enough, so have your way on this," Menzie withdrew to the kitchen. Mathew guarded the bottom of the stairs. The other men followed Menzie into the kitchen and closed the door.

Johanna ran with all her strength to Steven's house. She found him standing by his garden admiring the growth of the crops. Her chest hurt and heaved and her head spun as she leaned against him and blurted out what had happened. His arms were protectively about her as he calmed her and listened. His face stiffened in disbelief while a great calm came over him. He knew instantly what he must do. Steven had been waiting for this situation to arise. He supported Johanna into his house and made her take a glass of water. He collected his jacket and took his shotgun down from the wall. He looked at her to see if she was ready. She nodded and they left. He sent her to a phone box to call Gordon MacLeod, the island policeman, and to say that he, Steven, asked him to come. He walked on to the schoolhouse, feeling out the most skillful way to handle the house invasion.

Steven's history was steeped in the cruel enclosures that cleared islanders and sent them across the Atlantic. Many died as his people tried to resist. He remembered the powerlessness of his forefathers, their futile clinging to homes, subjected to the clearing of the landscape to make way for sheep enclosures. All this created layers of memory in his mind. It would never happen again while yet he lived.

He strode the distance to the schoolhouse and walked inside to find Mathew at the foot of the stairs. Helen was still playing in her bedroom shielded from what was emerging. He and Mathew looked at one another for a moment. Their silence was heavy with all that was unsaid. Mathew pale and cold, Steven filled with clarity and purpose that reached back into history. Mathew dropped his head to his chest in mute despair.

Steven gripped his shoulder, "No Mathew, not that. You must fight this and fight it skillfully. Fight it until it is finished. Otherwise these men have even more license to place their will and ways at the doors of other folk."

Mathew shook his head, knowing himself. "I'm not a fighter Steven, just an author who seeks peace." At Steven's silence he carried on. "I thought I had found it here, with you and on this island, but I was wrong." Steven raised him up gently but firmly and it was he, the old man, who had strength. He infused the young man with it.

Steven walked to the kitchen with Mathew behind him and opened the door. Menzie and the four men were sitting there, a half-eaten meal and a bottle of whisky on the table. John Menzie looked up at him and then studiously ignored him. Steven stood there surveying the ease and comfort of the men, their confidence, and still they ignored him while they continued their drinking and their eating. With one swift motion he swept the shotgun barrel along the table sending plates of food and bottle crashing to the floor to smash by an old dresser next to the fireplace. One man sprang to his feet only to find the shotgun pointed calmly, unwavering, at his stomach. They ignored him no longer, but Menzie remained unperturbed.

"Well, well Mr. Steven Martin, and what can we do for you this fine evening?" He was sure of himself and felt that he was in control of the situation.

Steven looked at him. He knew he had to intimidate the gathering.

"You can leave this place Menzie and not return."

Menzie laughed and sneered at him. "You're a stupid old fool Steven Martin. I've said that before and I'll say it again. You're a fool. I own this place and your friend there has no legal proof that he has any right to be here, so he goes at my whim. Do you see it plainly, now?" He grinned in the direction of his henchmen.

Steven quietly controlled his disdain of the man. "There are many things I see very plainly," he said. "I see your ignorance of this island. The law is not something we necessarily abide by. No family will ever be thrown from their house no matter the reason. Think well on that. Our forefathers were clubbed and driven from their homes and could not fight. Every generation since then has borne that stain and you would not leave this island in one piece if you evict this family."

Menzie laughed again and swore viciously at Steven, then found himself looking down the barrel of his shotgun. His composure was rattled by the tightening of the old man's finger on the trigger.

"You're dreaming old man. Half the people on this island are in my pocket. They owe me too many favours for money here and a chance at work there. It would be you they'll turn on if it comes to a choice."

Steven patiently stood there holding the men in thrall of him, keeping them in fear of what he might do. The policeman and Johanna found them so, locked and frozen in their history. Johanna quickly went upstairs to be with Helen. Gordon MacLeod had quickly responded to her call for help and had driven from the police station to her. He was not of this island, but a Highlander from Sutherland, huge, strong and implacable. Steven spoke quickly to him in Gaelic and lowered his gun. No one but he detected the glint of anger that flashed into the policeman's eyes.

"Is it a court order that you have Mr. Menzie for the moving of these people?" the constable asked courteously.

"I don't need one for my own house, constable. You can check that with my lawyer in Glasgow."

Gordon MacLeod pulled out his notebook and began writing laboriously with a pencil. He carefully watched the four men with Menzie from the corner of his eye. At any movement from them, he would look up from his writing and stare at them until they were still. He knew the violence in them. He could smell it, also their fear. He was a policeman but at this very moment his position lay as a thin veneer over his culture and history. He longed to spring at these men to meet their violence with his own. Outwardly he maintained an impassive calm as he questioned them, but they saw and knew that he desired only one chance to be at them. They denied him that chance. He then questioned Mathew and Johanna. At last he shut his notebook and returned the pencil to his pocket. He spoke gravely to Menzie.

"Mr. Menzie, you will leave this place and not return until you have a court order. If you do not leave I will take you and your men in to the police station."

Menzie jumped to his feet. "Don't be a fool MacLeod, you don't know the law. This has all been checked with my lawyer."

Gordon MacLeod retrieved his notebook and pencil and slowly stated aloud what he wrote: "Abusive language to a police officer." He stopped and snapped the book shut. His soft voice held a deadly menace." Mr. Menzie, on this island I am the law. Glasgow and your fancy lawyers have little influence here. Now what is it to be?" He fondled the truncheon at his belt, his fingers anxious to feel its weight swinging through the air.

Menzie was flustered and furious. "You're finished MacLeod. Your superintendent will hear of this and your days are numbered on the force."

"Is that so now Mr. Menzie? Are you threatening an officer of the law in addition to refusing to leave this place?" He took a step towards Menzie knowing that Steven would cover the other men. They saw the shotgun rise and motion them away from Menzie and the policeman. Gordon MacLeod was smiling and waiting. It was he that now had command of the situation. Menzie backed away and saw it was hopeless to argue. He did not want the policeman's hands on him.

"We'll go," he said harshly "But you've not heard the last of this." He made to leave but Gordon MacLeod called him back, notebook in hand.

"Threatening an officer" he wrote. "Will you be clearing up this mess you've made of the kitchen?"

"No damn you, no!" shouted Menzie, beside himself with frustration at the soft calm voice that civilly mocked him.

Gordon MacLeod pursed his lips and muttered "Breach of the peace" and resumed his laborious writing. Menzie whirled on his men and shouted at them to clear everything up, and stood watching in fury as they reluctantly bent to the task. Then they left and drove away.

There was a long silence as they listened to the sound of the van driving away. Gordon MacLeod let out a long breath that was almost a sigh of regret then looked at Steven. The old man chuckled, and the big policeman smiled back, "Bye, I could have cracked their skulls."

"Och Gordon, are you not a wee bit old for such exploits?"

"And yourself?" Gordon questioned, pointing a huge finger at the shotgun held loosely in Steven's hands.

"Is it this you mean?" Steven raised the gun to the window and pulled the trigger. Everyone winced and braced themselves for the explosion, but there was only a loud click as the hammer came down on the empty chamber.

"I was not about to waste cartridges on the likes of Menzie, was I now?"

Gordon MacLeod's mouth gaped open in surprise and soon he was chuckling with the old man as though they shared a special secret, which indeed they did. Johanna fetched whisky and glasses in the relief and they drank while they relived the evening. Gordon MacLeod rose to go. He was serious for a moment after he shook hands with Mathew and Johanna, his huge fist enveloping theirs in his strength and kindness.

"Menzie will be back and he'll have his court order. Don't think he won't. It will take two weeks or so but he'll get it. Then you must go. You understand now?"

They nodded at this bull of a man whose protection they had received. "Can they stay with you, Steven?" he asked.

Steven spread his hands in an expansive gesture. "My house is there waiting for them. They'll come home with me tonight if they wish."

"No, Steven, not this night." It was Mathew speaking slowly and deliberately. "We'll stay here until the court order arrives and then we'll leave only when it suits us."

Steven and Gordon smiled at him with a new admiration. And so they stayed. The words and rumours that flew from the events of that evening spread to many quarters of life. A magistrate sitting in a small town in the Highlands found technical reasons to delay and frustrate the granting of the court order that Menzie and his lawyer sought. And people from the island were kind to the young family, knowing they had felt the same hand of tyranny that their forebears had suffered under. But Mathew and Johanna were unhappy at the schoolhouse as there was a pall over it. Bitterness crept into their tongues and thoughts. So they left of their own accord and arrived at Steven's door one rain-driven evening and Mathew once again asked for shelter. They were expected and Steven opened his house and heart to them and tried to heal their hurt and disappointment.

# 4. Homecoming – Part Two

Menzie did return a month later armed with a court order, but his triumph was hollow as there was no one there to be removed.

He knew they were still on the island and it was inevitable that he and Mathew would meet. The islanders tensed, fearing the outcome. They had taken to Mathew and his family, yet feared what Menzie would do to him. The two men did meet - on a path that ran from the back of the central hills to the string of dunes that faced the Atlantic to the west. Neither had reason to be on the path but they had both been drawn to it upon that day.

 Menzie grinned to himself once he saw Mathew's slight figure approach. This would be easy, oh so easy. And it was. Mathew came steadily towards him and Menzie set himself to attack.

Mathew ducked the first blow, but could not avoid the foot that landed painfully in his stomach. He did not know how to fight but was no match for his powerfully built adversary. His punches glanced off Menzie as he was driven painfully backwards. He felt weak and sickened by a violence that was alien to him, but Menzie came on, relishing the pain he was handing out. Only once did he get careless and he stumbled as he aimed a kick at Mathew's groin. With a despairing rush Mathew ran into him and grappled him to the ground. With his remaining strength he seized Menzie by the hair and pounded his head into the ground. At seeing Menzie momentarily stunned and helpless, a remorseless rage swept over

Mathew and his sinews and muscles found new strength as he drove his fingers into Menzie's throat and started to throttle him.

Menzie's legs began to thrash as his system resisted the cutting of its lifeline. As his face turned red, suddenly there were Steven's strong hands also on his throat. He had followed Mathew, knowing there to be a portent in the day. He saw the two men meet and with a sinking heart he sat to watch the inevitable and prayed that his young friend would not suffer too much. He moved towards them only when Menzie lay stunned and inert with Mathew astride him choking the life from him. His fingers closed over Mathew's and he slowly loosened the grip on Menzie's throat.

"No Mathew, this is not your way." His firm insistence seeped through Mathew's blood fused mind. "This is not the way," he repeated as he released Menzie's neck from the vice-like grip that was crushing life from him. Mathew stood, breathing heavily, glittering a hatred for the coughing, wheezing man that writhed before him.

"Mathew," Steven spoke sharply, bringing him back to sanity. Mathew nodded, his limbs trembled at the strain and horror of what he had almost done.

"Mathew, it is not this way that you kill men such as Menzie. This is too easy for them." Mathew turned in surprise at the harshness in the old man's voice. "You destroy creatures like this not by killing them but by making of your own decency and goodness a monument for him to see. You must be a constant living rebuke to his lies and rottenness. So while he yet lives and knows you, he will be twisted and torn at seeing you. This he cannot abide, can you now Menzie?" He stepped to where Menzie lay, almost recovered. He placed his boot on

Menzie's throat and pressed until the man choked and gasped once more.

"Is it this way that we will kill you Menzie?" He released his boot so that the man could cough and splutter and fight for air.

"You understand me, do you not? We will let you go and live, so that you may be destroyed by your own black and twisted hate. It will turn inwards on you and be a lingering death while yet you live."

Steven's eyes were very calm as he delivered his words to Menzie. He stood and stared at him for a while then spat on the ground beside him, a gesture untypical of him, but one that was clearly understood. He turned away from him and took Mathew by the arm and they walked away to bathe the young man's cuts and bruises. Menzie stared woodenly at their retreating figures. He knew fear for the first time in his life, not of Steven but of himself.

Steven and Mathew made a slow progression home, the one supporting the other, talking of fencing and crops, the play that Mathew was writing as if nothing had happened. It was their good fortune that Johanna and Helen were not at the farm house. Steven tended to Mathew's hurts. They were both amused at the mosaic of sticking plaster, cuts and black eyes. Steven's thoughts were far off and he sifted words in his mind before speaking.

"Do you recall the land on my farm by the bay, the flat piece that smiles to the sea and catches all the sun?"

Mathew nodded.

"It would be a place for a house if there were builders."

Mathew shrugged, "I suppose so, what do you need another house for?"

"I'll not be needing another place. This one suits me well enough, but are you not looking for a place on this island?" Mathew stared at him, unbelieving. "It's not me that's wanting a place Mathew, it's you, Helen and Johanna. You'll have to do the building of it."

Mathew's mind was fuddled and slow to react. He had resigned himself to the leaving of this island and dreaded to part with Steven and the realms of experience they explored. "Do you mean this?" he asked, incredulous.

"Aye, I do. It will be our monument to decency, our rebuke and denial to Menzie's ilk." Steven's voice was intense and urgent. "It will be by the water where Helen first swam and where Johanna hooked a fish. You and your family will be safe from everyone - but me." He glowered in a mock fierceness as he humoured Mathew.

"I can't believe it." Mathew did not know what else to say.

Steven continued "There's a month left to the summer, time enough to get the foundations laid. We can start again in the spring, once the worst of winter is past."

Without words Mathew got to his feet and put his hand upon Steven's shoulder. He had received so much from this old man, how could he take any more.

Steven read his thoughts and shook his head. "You can chase that look from your eyes. This thing is for me as much as for you. There's a mountain of work for us to do."

Johanna and Helen burst in. They had heard of the fight while shopping in the main village and had hurried home.

Helen picked flowers to heal his hurts but Mathew was there smiling but battered as Johanna came into his arms and hugged him. Steven gravely accepted the flowers that Helen held towards him for her father.

"We're to build a house by the bay, Johanna." Mathew had no words to spare on his recent violence.

She smiled impishly at him, "Didn't you know? Steven's been planning that ever since he learned we were to buy the schoolhouse."

Steven tried to step outside to hide his deception, but Mathew's glance caught him and held him and then they were smiling together and holding one another by the shoulders. They were happy yet again.

*****

They worked hard in that final month of summer, hurrying and straining to complete the foundations of the new house before the first gale of winter would halt their efforts. It was to be a long, one-storied stone house with large windows facing the sea. They built from plans and their imagination and finished the foundation before winter. It was left to settle until spring while Mathew and his family returned to Cumberland.

John Menzie was also at work. Many men were indebted to him. His business success in Glasgow gave him the power and wealth to let people survive if he should choose to do so. It quickly became known that his disfavour would come to any man or woman who helped in the building of the place for Mathew and Johanna.

It was as innocents that the young family returned in the spring of the next year. They and Steven started to raise their monument to integrity and decency. They worked to put up the main framework. They laboured for several months and only slowly did they learn of the forces arrayed against them. The promised help from carpenters to put on a roof and from other tradesmen was not forthcoming. The driver of the one truck on the island could never find the time to carry the timbers and building materials from the pier. Slowly Steven understood. He went to them, his people, and gently asked why. Their discomfort and defiance moved him to a rare compassion. Steven told Mathew and Johanna in simple terms what was happening. They were unhappy and miserable. They told him of the turning away of people they had come to know in previous years. The snubs and whispers that seemed to follow them.

Steven was silent for a while as they sat there in despondency. "This thing against you will last for only so long," he explained to them. "In the minds of the islanders is fear for the future. Soon, very soon they will reassert themselves and you will see and share their goodness. It is Menzie they despise and will be rid of him. Do not ask too much of the people here, too quickly. Try to know and feel their ways."

They did not answer him and Steven tried to bring them to a different tack. "We must bring workers from the mainland to help us in the building, and we can finish what we have started here."

Mathew reached out to him, "Steven, for once I believe you to be wrong. We don't belong here. Just our being here has brought about a terrible train of events - violence, hate and suspicion. We came to find peace and beauty and met ugliness and fear. Johanna and I have talked of this. It hurts us that we should be shunned. What kind of person is it that will take his cue from Menzie? No Steven, we belong with you but not here."

Steven had waited for this moment, "Is there no patience on you, my young friends? Can you not be open to consider that your views are misplaced? That time has a way of resolving matters?"

Mathew shook his head stubbornly. "It's not lack of patience or lack of courage Steven. If we belonged here then nothing could ever move us away, but I'll not fight shadows in a place that has no promise for me."

Johanna had been listening to her two men and feared a break in their continuity. "We must leave here Steven," she said quietly, "but we cannot leave you. We want you to come with us, to live with us. It would be too painful else." She bit her lip to stop her tears.

Steven was grateful for her words. "Thank you Johanna for the asking. You know I cannot leave this place. But understand this thing. The island people who oppose me do so out of love. It is love meshed with bitterness and fear at being in this place and subject to every man's indifference. They cling fiercely to their own. They need the example of those that are young, true and brave, In the passing of time they will share their richness with you. But I know it is difficult for you to believe this. Time would show you differently." He paused for a moment, and then said, "I cannot convince you of this and so our words merely chase one another. Come Mathew, let us walk together."

The two men left, grateful for silence. Mathew felt the first fingers of impending disaster touch him, yet Steven stayed calm so they could remain free of this dread. They walked to the bay. Dug their toes in the sand newly washed by the tide and came at last to where they had worked. Frame timbers rose gaunt and stark from the foundation they had laid, and poked into the evening's sky as a rebuke to their unfinished labour of love and bravery.

"There's our monument to decency," said Mathew bitterly.

Steven remained calm and comforting. His heart had knowledge of what was to be drawn to that place. Mathew was as a son, his spirit was vital to him. His leaving would wound and scar, for it would leave bigotry and stealth the masters. The island folk would remember and miss him and later build on his memory and regret his leaving. How could this be said to a man who wished no longer to understand? It could not. It was the only way Mathew could face their parting. Just Steven's knowing remained.

The few days remaining before Mathew, Johanna and Helen departed the island, stretched slowly in the old man's mind. It was a quiet house that once they had made so joyful. Then it was over. Mathew cried openly as he took his leave and could not speak, so he turned away. Johanna came to Steven and cradled his old, graceful head in her arms and gently embraced him. They had booked a cabin and a passage for him on the ferry boat lest he should come. She whispered this through her tears knowing he could not.

He endured their pain in silence as his Helen now sat by him. Scarce three years since he had played his accordion for her. A whole lifetime of living in that slow stretching of time. She sat still and composed, not understanding the maelstrom of emotions swirling about her. Steven looked at her steadily. He looked deep into her eyes and saw that her heart was strong and brave and clutched her to him as she smiled at him. She laid her head on his chest and scarce felt the tears that fell to her head. Steven wept silently in joy. He had not lost her.

They left and he walked to the place where he could catch a sight of the ferry. He sat there and waited for the large boat to pass through the sound and make its way eastward to the mainland. He saw it pass and watched it fade into the horizon, for the last smudge of smoke to disperse and disappear into the clouds. He was quiet and confident at their leaving. On that point, graced by gulls and gentled by the sea, he held them close in his heart and knew peace. He slowly walked home and entered his house and stood by the window that looked to the east.

# Epilogue

The song of Steven continued.

It was never too late for him.

His knowing crept forth from him

to shock his people into new awareness.

And they were good people, bred from generations

of adversity and survival.


He fashioned it into creativity

by quiet gentle example that could not be denied.

The raw primacy of sea, rock and gale

let them turn only a little away,

allow just a brief lesion on that creative body of survival

that stretched back to the time before Antiquity.


They came in one's and two's to where Steven

and the young ones had started their work.

They looked and measured many things

in their minds and hearts.

Leaving, only to return in one's and two's.

It was the postman that trimmed the founds,

carrying cement on his back from the roadside,

where his bicycle lay with a wheel spinning in the wind.

A shipwright from the sea laboured on his leave

from the sea to put a roof to the place.

They finally could laugh

when the butcher, barman and pier master

came with separate carefully carpentered doors

all for the same doorway.

With the smiles that spread to a chuckle

and swelled to a roar of laughter,

the pain from deep within the breasts of island folk eased

as they became part of it all.

They felt the deep lasting joy of being

ensnared by a thread of life

that ran back to that time before Antiquity.

They heard and felt the song of Steven

rejoicing in their hearts.

# 5: Death of Eagle Speaker

Trailing Sky Six Feathers was uneasy about her husband's intent to journey to a distant outpost of soldiers north east of their village.

She anticipated that their livelihood would be compromised by intruders who did not care about their way of life. She could sense the damage and carnage done to other villages and knew they would not be avoided. And the growth of their livelihood would be abandoned.

As the central chief of The People in the latter part of the 18th century, Eagle Speaker accomplished many great things. He created a strong structure of clan chiefs who oversaw the managing of irrigation for their crops, and established the woman's council to regulate the planting and harvesting cycle essential for their culture and habitat.

Trailing Sky ensured that both men and women drew on the wisdom of the Earth Mother for their planting and harvesting. She and the women elders taught the importance of the plant and animal species – that there was wisdom and guidance to reckon with. Their well-being required such a natural law to sustain their existence. In this manner the women constantly restored the land they worked. Eagle Speaker made the voice of the women equal to that of the men, and they were also trained diligently to shoot with long rifles and how to fight in hand-to-hand combat. Their tribe was a confident and capable cadre of warriors ready to defend themselves.

Over the years, The People had grown strong with a reputation as a dangerous and well-organized enemy. Eagle Speaker created alliances with five regional tribes for mutual co-operation in times of conflict. Gradually he and Trailing Sky brought peace to the internecine warfare that characterized inter-tribal relations in the American Northeast. Through Trailing Sky, a medicine woman, Eagle Speaker rooted himself in a deep spiritual understanding and knowledge of the Earth Mother and was in tune with the Truth of the Creator.

Eagle Speaker was acutely aware of the encroaching presence of settlers and prospectors seeking homesteads to the far north of his village in the shadow of the military forts. The presence of American soldiers in distant forts had followed the trickle of homesteaders and prospectors north of their region. The military outposts were now a tangible fact of their lives though Trailing Sky and Eagle Speaker did not care for the disdain shown toward their people. They knew the settlers and soldiers were a force to be reckoned with.

Eagle Speaker intended to establish the rights of The People to the lands and territories required to sustain them. To do this, he knew he had to negotiate skillfully with the military leaders. He discussed his plan with Trailing Sky, and she shared with him her intuitions. She knew that a parley with the soldiers was necessary, yet felt a strong fear surrounding his journey.

In the prime of his life, Eagle Speaker set out to the distant outpost of soldiers. Eagle Speaker brought the same skills he had developed with fractious Indian nations to bear on the presence and demands of the military. He took four of his finest horses to trade with the soldiers at the outpost. To his dismay, he was met with desolation at the military fort. The soldiers and the Indians gathered there were ill and dying from cholera. He rode past unburied bodies of Indians placed in one corner of the compound. Soldiers were dead in their billets. The officer in command waved him away so he would not get contaminated, though he passed closely to the dead Indians. Eagle Speaker left his four fine horses with the commander as a token of goodwill for future negotiations and began his journey home. As he was riding he came upon a fallen Indian. He dismounted to help him only to find him dead. He travelled on and saw a few more and then a pile of bodies.

The first part of his journey home was uneventful but soon he began to feel dreadfully weak and sick. As he travelled further from the outpost, severe chills overwhelmed him. He vomited frequently and felt the life force draining from his body. The effects of cholera at the outpost had infected him. He fell several times from the back of his horse as his strength faded; the last time while crossing a river. He fought to reach the river bank, hanging on to his horse's tail and hauled himself up to the base of a weeping willow tree by the river's edge. There he lay, soaked, shivering with fever coursing through his body.

Eagle Speaker realized he was less than a day's ride from The People's main settlement. He released his faithful mare, urging the horse home to bring Trailing Sky to the willow tree. The horse ran fast and true so that by nightfall she was breathing hard beside Eagle Speaker's dwelling place in the village. Trailing Sky, hearing the mare, instantly knew that something terrible had taken place.

With a sinking heart, Trailing Sky gathered her medicines and sent her daughter Rising Moon to fetch two fresh horses and to also alert the Clan Chiefs who followed shortly afterwards. Trailing Sky rubbed Eagle Speaker's mare down with a soft deerskin and gave her food and water as she talked to the creature asking her to guide them to Eagle Speaker. As she asked the horse to lead her to her husband, she knew already he was dying, yet she was not ready to let him go. She silently prayed to her spiritual mentors, the Sky People, to keep him alive and to help her reverse the death process. She could not bear to lose him at this time of their life.

Rising Moon arrived with fresh horses. Trailing Sky rode Eagle Speaker's mare and only switched to the horse brought by her daughter when she felt the mare tiring. They rode northward through the forests and to another plateau before descending eastward to the river's edge. The rays of the full moon as it cast light on the trees did little to dispel the darkness around and within them. The majestic buttes were etched beautifully by the moonlight, a contrast to the dark canyons across the river. They stopped frequently to enable the mare to rest. At these periodic breaks, Trailing Sky and Rising Moon spoke earnestly to one another.

"Mother, what medicines do we need for Father?"

"I have all that may be needed." Trailing Sky replied

Rising Moon was listening to her mother. She smiled at how they had often referred to her father as "Little Sister" as he was always ready to learn from Trailing Sky's skill in ceremonial matters. On that long, dreadful, dark night an understanding grew in Rising Moon's heart about her parents, as she came to fathom the depth of thought and organization that went into the renewal of their community.

The landscape they travelled through that night had a rare beauty and stillness. It felt as though time itself had stopped - perhaps a portent of things to come. A foreboding rebuke to the crisis they already knew they were to face together. By daybreak they found Eagle

Speaker, near to death with fever, underneath the weeping willow tree, whose branches touched lightly onto the river's surface. Trailing Sky knew what to do with the fever to prevent it from infecting her and The People. She asked Rising Moon to fetch water from the river so her medicines could be prepared. She noticed an ancient medicine wheel on a high bluff overlooking the canyon to the east, just above the weeping willow tree where they had found Eagle Speaker. She knew this was where she must take him to summon the Sky People to help her. The two women quickly built a frame to carry him to the medicine wheel. Support was immediately at hand as the Clan Chiefs with twenty warriors arrived. They had carefully followed the tracks left by the two women. Trailing Sky asked the Clan Chiefs to carry her husband to the medicine wheel on the carrying frame, which she and Rising Moon had hastily constructed.

The Clan Chiefs gently laid the frame on the medicine wheel so that Eagle Speaker's head was in the west, his heart in the centre and his feet pointing to the eastern door of the medicine wheel. The eastern door was where the Sky People could enter from the Universe. Trailing Sky mixed her medicines with appropriate prayers, yet by this time she knew that even her medicinal powers were insufficient. She called on the Sky People to save her husband, as they had long been her mentors. Their extraordinary energy could be felt entering from the canyon to the east and then spreading up to the medicine wheel into which Eagle Speaker had been placed. But Eagle Speaker was too far gone for even their extraordinary powers. Trailing Sky felt a momentary rush of rage at the inability of the Sky People to help her save Eagle Speaker, but she knew that her rage merely covered her grief and deep sorrow. She abandoned it immediately and asked for forgiveness from her mentors, requesting the Sky People to help her face the ordeal of her husband's death.

She then lit four fires of sacred herbs within each quadrant of the medicine wheel to purify him for his journey across time and space. She had prepared herbs and medicine long ago for such an instance. With some water from the river, brought up by Rising Moon, she held his head so he could drink it. Eagle Speaker came back to her for a moment and smiled. It was a smile so beautiful it enveloped her with so much love that Trailing Sky almost broke down. She instantly remembered their first meeting, the silent young warrior offering her a bundle of feathers at a trading parley between her people and Eagle Speaker's people. He did not speak and did not smile on that occasion, yet here he was dying in her arms. It was almost too much for her. She had to hang on to her knowledge as a medicine woman and what she now had to do. Her grief and deep sorrow abated, and she summoned inner strength and love to assist Eagle Speaker in the journey his spirit would take to cross time and space. She beseeched the Sky People to enable her to stay steady and for Eagle Speaker to journey safely.

His eyes opened once more and he asked if Rising Moon was there. And there she was, tears pouring down her beautiful face.

"Do not cry my daughter. I am going to the Sky People and will watch over you and your mother from there."

"I am here Father, right beside you with mother."

Trailing Sky stopped preparing her medicines for a moment. Very softly she said, "Husband, you are still with me. I do know where you are going next."

He smiled beautifully to her and raised his hand to touch her. She gently held his arm.

"I have done all I can my husband and do not know if I can continue."

Eagle Speaker said, "You must continue Trailing Sky Six Feathers. I can see you now just as when I first was silenced by your beauty and majesty. I gave you six feathers because I could not speak."

His voice gave her strength and she quietly sang his favorite ceremonial chant. As his eyes closed again she whispered to Rising Moon, "I still have the six feathers at home and will give them to you as a gift from your father."

By this time family groups from the village continued to arrive until there was over one thousand of The People gathered at the high bluff where their leader now lay in the centre of the medicine wheel. The Clan Chiefs had alerted all the families, and they came, leaving only the elderly and sufficient caretakers of their village behind. The families were quiet, knowing that this was not a usual death, but something deeply profound. The Clan Chiefs and Rising Moon stood in silence round the medicine wheel. They were in awe of Trailing Sky's calm and fortitude. Only she knew of her inward struggle and sorrow. She surmounted both successfully and began to chant the sacred songs of her people. As she sang, Eagle Speaker looked up at her for the last time with the same amazement he had done so often during their life together. Just before he drew his last breath, she cradled his head in her arms, leaned over and whispered softly so that no one would hear.

"I will find you, my husband. I will find you."

As Eagle Speaker began to travel on universal waves, Trailing Sky chanted the sacred song of the Sky People, the secret chant that saved their lives before. She chanted their journey to the cave, to their care for the Earth

Mother and for The People. Sharing at last in her husband's smile she cried tears of pure joy to accompany the chant. She continued chanting throughout the night to prevent her grief from overwhelming her. The Clan Chiefs and family groups stayed close to her. On the dawn of the second day, Rising Moon, who had sat quietly outside the medicine wheel, approached her mother. She gently took her mother's arm and whispered, "It is time mother."

Rising Moon had expected her mother to be gaunt and drained by grief. Instead she gasped in surprise at the radiance of her mother's face, framed as it now was by long, white hair. The ordeal of her husband's transition had turned Trailing Sky's black tresses to snow. She looked majestic as she gently laid her husband's head down from the cradle of her arms.

Trailing Sky stood and looked around at The People gathered on this high bluff above the gentle river. She lifted her arms to the sky as if she were holding him still. Rising Moon stood beside her and did the same. All the People raised their arms at the same time, to the sky and to the universe. Then they heard Trailing Sky's strong voice,

"We will prepare my husband's body in the old way, for all our relations and the Earth Mother."

She asked the Clan Chiefs to build a platform for Eagle Speaker's body, so that his body could be offered to the elements in the same way as his grandfather's body before him. The burial platform was constructed swiftly with vines strung across to carry the weight of Eagle Speaker's body. The platform was placed next to the medicine wheel on the West side following Trailing Sky's instructions. Crow Feather, chief of the North Clan, had brought with him a freshly cured bear skin. He brought this to Trailing Sky, knowing that it would be needed.

She thanked Crow Feather for his gift and gently wrapped her husband's body with the bear skin, remembering that this was done for Eagle Speaker's grandfather when he met his death.

Very tenderly the Clan Chiefs carried Eagle Speaker's body to the platform that they had erected. Its outline against the sky was stark at the top of the high bluff above the weeping willow tree and river, with the dark canyon stretching to the east.

The fingers of the dawn had drawn daylight awake so everyone could see. The medicine women had strung vines of forest flowers, herbs and grasses around the four strong posts. Trailing Sky climbed the notched pole that was the ladder to where her beloved lay. She was humming a chant to herself as she lovingly laid his favorite bow, arrow and spear by his side. She placed her medicine pouch in his clasped hands in front of his body, so that he would have sustenance for his next journey.

When she descended the notched pole and asked the chiefs to remove it, Trailing Sky requested that they return in six months to take the platform down and render to ashes anything that was left of Eagle Speaker. The ash was to be scattered to the four directions, into the river and into the sky. Then she took her place in front of the funeral place of her husband and faced The People. She stood tall, magnificent and powerful before the thousand members of The People who had followed the path to this moment. All those gathered sensed her extraordinary power. In a steady measure she began to chant the life story of her beloved Eagle Speaker, from what she remembered him speaking of and from what she knew of him. Her voice was strong and melodious and it was taken in to every listener's heart.

The People swayed backwards and forwards in a spontaneous dance that had its own unison. They clasped arms around shoulders that shook with grief as they danced forward and backward to the mesmerizing chant Trailing Sky offered to them. She chanted the circumstances of Eagle Speaker's birth and his naming after the great eagle by his grandfather. Her voice carried the story of Eagle Speaker's training with his grandfather in the mountains, desert and forests of their region and how Eagle Speaker came to live his life in constant prayer. She sang blessings for his mother and father and for all who nurtured him. She sang the story of her first meeting with this handsome young man who moved with the grace of a mountain lion; of how he named her with his gift of six feathers, of how their eyes had connected that first time as if drawn together by the threads of time.

Strong warriors bowed their heads and wept openly as her vibrant voice shook everyone to their core. Other warriors fell to their knees, overwhelmed by the burden of loss. Rising Moon, distraught, leaned on the woman warrior Dancing Mountain Lion, who stood strong while the tears poured down her cheeks. The People were then uplifted from their sorrow when the chant from Trailing Sky carried everyone to remember all that Eagle Speaker had put in place for The People and the legacy that they must cherish and build upon.

Trailing Sky chanted about the first deadly raid on their summer settlement and their retreat to the cave in the sacred canyon. She continued with the story of his wise preparation for the later raid, of how Eagle Speaker had orchestrated the changes that built The People stronger. She sang of his wisdom and patience that wove a tapestry of co-operation between clans and peoples. She chanted of their daughter, Rising Moon, the exquisite bond between daughter and father, and the tenderness he always showed to both of them. Then Trailing Sky's voice fell silent for a moment. After a time that stretched painfully into infinity, she announced to all with a voice that now had a power they were not expecting, "I am Trailing Sky Six Feathers. I ask you all to witness my last words to my husband, Eagle Speaker, before he died in this medicine wheel on the high bluff above the river."

It was as though every one of The People took a deep breath at the same time, waiting for Trailing Sky's next words,

"As he smiled to me and took his last breath, I said to Eagle Speaker, I will find you my husband, I will find you."

The ensuing silence cut through everyone's tension, fear and grief. The words that had been heard by Eagle Speaker, now voiced by Trailing Sky for The People, was taken by a whisper of wind into every heart.

The trees heard her words and told the animals and birds. The clouds heard her words and extended them to the Sky People.

Across the forests, grasslands and mountains, her words echoed, growing stronger and more penetrating so that the universe itself paused to listen.

On hearing her mother's words, Rising Moon gasped out loud in emotional pain as tears poured down her face. Then she was very still, swaying like a sapling in the morning breeze. She cried out, "Mother, will I find him too?"

Trailing Sky gently took her beautiful daughter's tear streaked face in her two hands and said, "Yes my daughter. Eagle Speaker has traveled safely. We will both find him.

# 6: Echoes From Before

Several decades ago I became aware that I had a stalker.

I would glance over my shoulder. Then feel a distinct presence that persisted in following me.

White Eagle Woman, my shaman mentor, made it clear I was mistaken. This was no stalker. It was a woman from the 18th century, a medicine woman from the American Southwest. She was trying to bring powerful medicine gifts to me in the 21st century. She had a name – Trailing Sky Six Feathers.

How did this come about?

The first time I became aware of her was when I was a young professor at Carleton University. I was splitting my time between Ottawa, Canada, and the Hebrides in Scotland trying to create an academic career, and, at the same time, save a failing marriage. I was not doing a good job with either.

In Ottawa I was a professor at Carleton University teaching anthropology. But in the Hebrides I was a mariner. I had a boat in the Hebrides, *An Dhoran* - a twenty six foot clinker built vessel, to enter the dangerous surrounding sea with tourists on board.

My teacher about the sea was Callum McAuley, a Master Mariner. He possessed a legendary knowledge of the tides, currents and landing places up and down the southern isles of the Outer Hebrides. At one time he had been skipper of the lighthouse tender, a boat that carried relief crews and supplies to the manned lighthouse on

Barra Head, an island at the southernmost tip of this island chain. His position with the lighthouse tender came to an end when a cargo ship, the S.S. Politician, was wrecked in a storm on the small islands off Eriskay. It had a full cargo of whisky destined for the US market. Callum swiftly used the lighthouse boat to take advantage of this unexpected windfall and managed to smuggle crates of whisky ashore and hide them from the Home Guard. He was apparently very successful at this chess game, which is the reason he was relieved of his post on the lighthouse tender.

Callum became my mentor of the sea and crewman on *An Dhoran*. I would listen to his fascinating stories as we pored over his charts. His presence on board my small boat brought his vast knowledge back to life. After more than forty years ashore, he was back in his natural element. It was always a struggle to keep him sober for the charter trips, but, by and large, he would time his drinking binges with the days when I was not putting out to sea.

It was on this boat that I sensed another life force at work. One disastrous sea journey still scars my mind to this day. It was from Eriskay, an island to the north, back to my home on the island of Barra.

Before leaving Eriskay, I checked the weather forecast. A storm and fog warning was predicted for later that evening, and I estimated that we would be home well before it descended. I had four tourists on board, as well as my oldest child. Iain was eleven years old at that time.

The voyage across the stretch of sea separating Eriskay from Barra was uneventful. As I started to navigate down the east coast of Barra, I slammed into the unanticipated storm and dense fog. The weather quickly morphed into gale force winds making it impossible to return to Eriskay.

There was no place to shelter on the east coast of Barra. I knew the fierce sea conditions in the Minch, the stretch of sea that separates the islands from the mainland of Scotland, so I stayed close to the east coast of the island.

The force of the storm was much more powerful than my twenty-five horsepower engine. The gale swept the ocean swells to break over the prow of my boat. Sharp spray from the sea struck my face like pellets from a shotgun.

I shielded my face with one arm to better see the huge waves coming right at the boat. I manoeuvred *An Dhoran* so she was at an angle to the waves and could crest over the swells rather than be battered to pieces.

My son, Iain, used the boat hook to fend off the trailing dinghy from smashing into the stern of the boat. I felt myself entering a terrible, cold silence while braced at the wheel. There was no thinking mind there, only an intuitive awareness of danger in this moment, then danger in the next moment.

Navigation was just far enough away from the inshore spurs of rock jutting out like razors. I stood quietly at the wheel muttering the 23rd Psalm, "I shall not want."

I turned *An Dhoran* through a narrow gap in an offshore rock spur. I caught a swell as it crested through the gap, spinning the wheel hard to port to avoid the ragged edge of another rock ledge, then quickly to starboard to find a more sheltered stretch of sea. This sort of maneuver was beyond my capabilities. I did not have that knowledge. I did not have that skill. This was not something I had learned from Callum McAuley. My mind simply did not operate, yet I had a seamless connection to a furious sea. A powerful instinctive knowledge took over as I felt an ethereal female presence guiding me through.

My friends on Eriskay, on seeing the worsening weather, had quickly telephoned the houses and crofts on the east coast of Barra and asked the townsfolk to turn on every light. Their urgent message was:

*"Prattis left Eriskay an hour ago and is across the sound. He cannot turn back in this storm. Needs all your lights switched on to help him navigate."*

With relief, I noticed the lights bordering the coastline and that gave me navigation marks to get back to Castlebay. I directed the frightened tourists to sit inside the cabin to add weight at the front end of the boat. This extra ballast saved the timbers of our vessel from being split open as the sea smashed into the creaking clinker boards.

I sensed something else with its hands on the wheel. The slow progress down the coastline of Barra continued under a mantle of desperate prayers. Finally, we came slowly into the sheltered harbour of Castlebay. My wife paced the dock as we arrived to gather Iain and take him home. The phone call that we were rounding the tip of Barra brought her to the harbour with blankets for my son and a fierce glare for me. We were not on good terms. The other passengers disembarked with great relief.

I moored *An Dhoran* at her berth in the bay next to the Castle. The wind was dropping and the fog had begun to clear. Callum and I rowed to shore in the dinghy, then with ropes pulled it back to its mooring place. It sat there gently bobbing across from the Post Office and the small boat pier. Callum had been totally silent throughout the journey from Eriskay, which was most unlike him. He had been watching me. And praying. Callum McAuley, Master Mariner, said to me in a shaky voice, "Ian boy, I don't know how the hell you did that. In all my years, I have never seen anything like it."

"Callum, I don't know how I did that either," I replied in a hoarse, bewildered whisper.

It became even more mysterious when the news reported that the storm had spared my small boat but had taken down a large trawler in the middle of The Minch. Then I said, "Callum, you're coming with me to the Castlebay Bar."

Callum shook his head and reminded me that he had been banned from the bar for twenty years now.

"Not tonight," I grimly said. He looked at me with a touch of both fear and amazement as we walked up the hill to the Castlebay Bar. Callum was reluctant to step inside and as soon as he did, Roddy the bartender came over to throw him out.

"Roddy, he's with me tonight," I said. There was something steely in my voice that caught Roddy's attention. He paused for a moment as he had already heard about our journey from Eriskay. News travels fast on the island. He looked from Callum to me and then reluctantly nodded his consent.

Callum was quickly surrounded by some of his seafaring friends eager to hear him tell the story. I greeted his cronies, who were delighted at this rare occasion. I placed two ten-pound notes on the counter. The sum total of my earnings from a day of insanity on the sea.

"Roddy, this will cover me tonight."

Roddy's large hand held out a glass tumbler, which he had filled with his best whisky.

"We'll not be taking your money, my friend. Everyone is relieved you are back safely." My hands shook as I took the first glass of whisky from Roddy's huge fist.

A long row of full whisky glasses appeared on the wooden bar I was wearily leaning against. Callum told and retold the story of the day's journey on *An Dhoran,* each time more elaborate than the previous telling. I did not listen. My mind was frozen. I knew that it was not me who brought the boat home safely.

At closing time, I thanked Roddy for allowing Callum his night of storytelling and walked over to the table where he was taking our voyage into mythological realms. Perhaps that was where it belonged. Callum still had a full glass of whisky in front of him.

"Time to go Callum, maybe you don't need that final shot."

"Indeed, I do," he replied with as much dignity as he could muster.

"I could be dead tomorrow, so there's no point in leaving it sitting here, is there now." He downed it and I helped him out of his chair. He sang and fell over a few times as we walked to the small cottage he shared with his sister Morag. He continued to tell me the story of the voyage as though I did not know the details of it.

I eventually delivered him to his cottage and coaxed him into his comfortable armchair, where he promptly fell asleep.

I walked to my home, overlooking the bay. It was calm and peaceful, nothing like the earlier hours on the sea. I could see the Castle and the islands to the south shrouded by the soft light from the quarter moon.

Sitting on the steps of my house, I mulled over the dangerous day. My reflections were savage, yielding ugly truths long buried. I thought of the line of whiskies at the bar, a celebration of returning from the furious sea. There was nothing to celebrate.

Rather, a rebuke was needed for my recklessness in endangering the lives of others, including my first-born son.

I could take no credit for bringing *An Dhoran* home. I thought of the sea as a piercing dirty grey, the color of dying. I knew I was not in the right place and did not belong here. I had obscured this reality with blind recklessness,

I was no heroic captain at the wheel, just stupid and displaced. I had to put an end to my madness on the sea. I suddenly realized that this beautiful island in the Hebrides was not where I was to be. The stressful drain on time and energy travelling back and forth between Canada and the Isle of Barra was debilitating. It left me with zero life-force energy for the work I was destined to do – particularly as a writer. It was time to move on as I was surviving amidst the suffering of being totally misplaced. So down I went into the graceless oblivion that alcohol and depression permits

I stood up slowly and stepped into my house. Still in the grip of that awful, chilling silence, I stretched out on the large sofa in the kitchen. My border collie Bruce crept over and rested his chin on my chest to provide comfort. I knew I had to drastically change the course of my life and emerge from the swamp I had created. This deadly sea voyage and others just like it were the signal to embark on a deep spiritual journey. They were not my hands on the wheel.

On my return to Canada after that brutal summer, I met White Eagle Woman at an elders gathering. Her air of quiet authority immediately struck me. She looked into me deeply and saw that I needed help.

She had been instructed by her ancestors to train me, and it began straight away with an eight-day vision quest, a prelude to a thirty-year period of training and healing under her spiritual guidance. This allowed the mosaic of the past to reveal itself. She identified Trailing Sky Six Feathers for me and revealed the guardian role held by her.

White Eagle Woman also taught me how to create a medicine wheel in my mind. I was always to start by bringing into my mind the ancient shaman from the East, then the South, West and North in succession, finally to bring in the ancient shaman from the Centre. She instructed me to see this as a map in my mind. I was then told to call forth the animal guides I had personally experienced, again starting from the East. I had experienced many animal guides and told her so.

White Eagle Woman retorted with some exasperation: "Choose the most powerful ones, dammit!"

With that cryptic encouragement, I chose mountain lion in the East, moose in the South, deer in the West and medicine bear in the North, with dolphin and whale below and the great eagles above. The space at the centre of the mental medicine wheel was the sacred still-point, a conduit for me to dialog with Trailing Sky Six Feathers but only when connection to the sacred mystery was intact.

When I died in Trailing Sky Six Feathers' arms back in 1777, she vowed to find me in the future. She refused to give up on me regardless of how dense I was in present time. Through her insistent guidance, my karma was reversed. The internal battles ceased. I learned to navigate past and present life experiences over four centuries. The medicine gifts required that I nurture skills to use them wisely. A clear mosaic of experiences stretching back to 1777 became clear.

Once the Vision Quest with White Eagle Woman was complete, I carefully built the medicine wheel in my mind and then spoke to Trailing Sky about the sea journey.

"Trailing Sky, was it you that brought my boat safely home?" I already knew the answer.

"You were there on all the other dangerous voyages were you not Trailing Sky?" I said softly to her, affirming her guardian presence.

She responded after a long pause. "I had to keep you alive, your son too, for he receives the Torch after your passing. I kept you alive when you almost lost your right arm in a foolish fight in Vancouver. I also kept you alive when you were dying in India."

Flashing through my mind were all the moments when death had faced me in this lifetime. She had always been there whenever my life was at risk and brought me through to safety. I took our dialog to another level, "When I die, will you be there? What will happen to you?"

Her voice was soft and precise. "When you die, I will be the last portion of your consciousness to dissolve. Before that moment of dissolution I will guide both of us as one integrated mind into the next adventure."

I was stunned into a long silence and refrained from asking about the next adventure. Trailing Sky Six Feathers is not an illusion, a projection I am attached to. She constitutes all that is crystal clear and wise within me, the ultimate Muse. I stayed very quiet until it was late in the night. I knew she was listening to my thoughts. Just before midnight, she quietly said to me,

"You have transformed all that you brought in with you and suffered from in this life. The person who stumbled blindly through the first part of your life is not the Ian walking through the second part of life. In India, Arizona, France, the Canadian wilderness and around the world you went to extraordinary lengths to deal with karma. You changed course and now have freedom and alignment. There were so many severe experiences, but you responded by moving in a spiritual direction. You touched universal threads that allowed me to keep my promise from 1777. And we are both grateful for that."

I could feel her smile expand along with my own. I placed my two hands together with great reverence and offered a deep bow of gratitude to Trailing Sky Six Feathers.

Namaste.

85

# PRESENT

# 7: Solace of Winter

Donald breathed on the window glass to melt the frost and saw the fringe of ice skirting the bay on the island.

The bitterly cold wind from the north soughed along the shore, freezing everything it gripped. Snow lay in drifts, piled deep to the spine of the northern mountains.

The cold stole into every door, numbing the hands and minds of those unprepared for it. A mire of ice covered the windowpanes. Donald's clothes were unkempt. He pulls on his coat and scarf, stoops to the window to regard the day's weather then goes back to start the fire. The room was untidy and dirty with newspapers and dishes strewn about the place.

Breathing heavily he lit the fire, humming tonelessly to himself, indifferent to the squalor around him. In this, his sixty-eighth year, he simply did not care. No one came there and he chose not to go anywhere. His face was heavily lined, older than its years. His mouth pursed as he sucked at his teeth waiting for the fire to catch and grunted in pleasure as the flames grew.

He spread his large, weathered hands to catch their warmth and shuffled into the kitchen to coax a paraffin burner to life, placing a kettle of water on it to boil. Not even thinking of the day and what he had to do. His response to the seasons and their demands were automatic. He waited in his freezing kitchen for the boiling kettle, then took his cup and made tea, collecting a large spoon and a pot of cold stew from the pantry. His breakfast was the cold, greasy lamb stew and a large cup of tea.

His boots and socks were lined with newspapers, another layer placed between his shirt and jacket before he stepped outside as the cold hit him. He walked hurriedly to the barn.

The animals shuddered at the raw blast as the door opened but quickly recognized him. The hens boldly gathered about him as he talked to them, reaching to the loft for their feed and water, searching for their nesting places in the barn for their eggs. They offered large brown eggs to this man with the soft voice and gentle hands, before he took hay to his cow. He put the hay in the manger and ran his hand over her back and flanks. She lowed softly and turned to rub her head on his leg while he cleaned the manure from her stall and put fresh water in the trough.

The barn was cleaner than his house and some nights he would sleep there next to the sound and warm smell of his animals. The cow was milked with his strong fingers drawing milk from her swollen udders. He hummed a tune that he once danced to, drawing life and vigour from the company of beasts, and placed the two buckets, one with eggs, the other overflowing with milk, on a shelf by the door. Taking a half-filled sack of cobnuts he braced himself again for the cold.

He trudged away from the barn, searching for the dozen sheep he still kept, wondering where they would be sheltering. He climbed the ridge that separated his house from the rest of the deserted village, noticing clumps of moss underfoot and icicles hanging from fences. No smoke rose from any chimney. Fences hung in disrepair. Empty houses gave themselves to the ravages of time.

In the distance some four miles away he could make out the thin ribbon of the new road, built to take tourists more rapidly from one end of the island to the other, cutting off his village. He was the only one left. He preferred his solitude and isolation, warmed only by nature and animals. He had long ceased to think about the world he had turned his back on.

He saw his sheep huddled for warmth in the lee of a deserted farmhouse and picked his way through the snowdrifts towards them. The wind had dropped and the sweat from his body had turned his layers of newspaper to a spongy mass, so he threw them away. The sheep had seen him and galloped towards him, some floundering in drifts in their eagerness. He patiently dug them out and fed them by hand from the sack and led them to a deserted house and opened the door so that they could shelter there. He counted them. They were all there. Donald shivered as he sat there pressed against them for warmth. His sack was empty but still his creatures ferreted for more. He laughingly pushed them away and stood up to go, noticing a change in the sky that heralded more snow.

He wondered if the Canada Post van left his supplies by the road. The van came with groceries once a week. The driver would leave a box of bare essentials for the man he rarely saw, taking his dues from the monthly cheque from the district office that he cashed for Donald. The two men would exchange few words on the rare occasions they met but there was a subliminal trust between them. If Donald did not have money, he would leave a basket of eggs, a shoulder of mutton or a box of filleted fish and the van driver would arrive at an adequate recompense. This primitive form of barter suited both parties.

He walked the few remaining miles to the road leaving the sheep in the deserted house. Broken fence frames stuck out from the grip of the snow. Wooden sheep pens, broken and derelict, groaned with the ice expanding in their seams.

He arrived at the road and saw that a cardboard box had been left for him. He opened it and examined each article before putting them in his sack; flour, butter, sugar, tea, nails, cartridges, and a large pot of home-made jam. He smiled at this and muttered to himself, "Nice man that driver, must leave a salmon for him one of these days."

He transferred the sack to his back and began the walk home. His hands and feet were numb and his eyes stared as he gulped great breaths of air. Finally reaching his door, he fumbled with frozen fingers at the latch until it yielded to admit him. His fire was all but out though he had banked it with slow-burning peat. It had taken him longer to struggle to the road and back than he had anticipated. He took paper and thrust it under a still smouldering log.

His hands could not grip his box of matches and while he tried again and again to take a match between his fingers the paper took flame from the log. Gratefully he bent to it, placing small sticks round the flame, building it up to take wood stacked next to the hearth. The warmth shot through his hands like a pain as the cold thawed from him. He shuddered at the sensations in his body but did not move away until the flames cast their warmth to the room. He hung the pot of cold stew on a hook above the fire and added flour and salt to his greasy mixture.

While it cooked he went to the barn, to feed his animals and bring back the eggs and milk. He was tired as the cold had drained him. It was with relief that he finally closed his door for the night, stuffing paper and rags into the gaps through which winter's fingers would poke. An involuntary shiver passed through him as he sat on his bed before the fire.

His stew boiled, and he ate ravenously, spooning it straight from the pot to his mouth, soaking lumps of bread into the gravy and eating them with his fingers.

He carried the empty pot to the kitchen and took a long drink from the bucket of milk. It left a white stain around his lips which he wiped with his sleeve. Donald belched in satisfaction and wearily returned to the warmth. As the fire continued to burn he lay fully clothed on the bed and pulled the heavy blankets over him.

The winter seemed to never end. Donald was desperate for the spring to come. He needed the signs of continuity and life to guide him on his own peculiar struggle for survival. He had forgotten why he had become so separate from friends and family, if indeed any decision had consciously been made. He had clung to his father's barren farm, to the hills and his animals and they had nurtured him in a way that human company could not. He was not unhappy, neither was he happy - he was simply content to survive.

Donald stood by the road basking in the first signs of spring as the Canada Post van pulled up. The driver climbed out with a sack of provisions under one arm and a letter clutched in his other hand.

"Letter for you. All the way from Vancouver."

Though the deep cold of winter had thawed, allowing the first daffodils to poke their heads above ground with their yellow splendour - the thaw had not penetrated Donald. He stood uneasily in the spring sunshine, staring at the letter held out to him. He slowly took the envelope and a faint uneasy memory stirred in him as he recognized the writing.

"I believe it's from your sister," said the van driver.

Donald nodded in agreement and stood still for a moment as he wondered why she would write to him. He stuffed it into his pocket, collected his sack of provisions, and walked away from the van.

The driver shook his head slowly and reached out to collect the bucket of eggs left there for him. Behind the bucket was a box of clams. The driver again shook his head at the strangeness of the man he would have liked to know better.

There was turmoil in Donald's mind as he walked to his desolate home. Moira, his sister, thirty years since he had seen her, now writing to him. Her letter remained unread for several months, sitting underneath a cup on the mantelpiece.

He went about his daily round with his animals and salmon traps, taking care of the creatures that sustained him. He caught the changing tide in a small rowing boat he had salvaged. He carefully placed several traps by a rock skerry where he knew the first salmon of spring would be hiding.

But the letter from Moira kept drifting into his mind. It lay neglected on the mantle for most of the summer until he could stand it no longer and hurried home from the oar he was mending and he took the letter down. He opened it and read what Moira had to say, admiring the roundness of her script. She had been to the island several times but could never bring herself to cross the gulf that now separated sister and brother. She had seen him from the road. "So that was the well-dressed body who stared at me so long," mused Donald.

She wanted to see him. She was widowed and would come in late autumn. She did not expect that he would meet her at the ferry.

"No I wouldn't do that, right enough," he muttered to himself. She could make her own way.

He read the letter several times before placing it back underneath the cup. He rubbed his hand over the stubble on his chin and said to himself. "I must clean this place up and get used to shaving for when she comes."

He glanced round at the midden he inhabited and smiled ruefully to himself. He liked his walls and took comfort from the simple homeliness of the clutter. He talked and chuckled to himself as he imposed a certain tidiness and cleanliness to his home. All for his sister's visit in Autumn.

He was harvesting his main crop of potatoes when he saw her walk from a car that stopped at the road. The smells and sounds of that morning had pleased Donald as he waited for Moira. He cocked his head to listen to the different songs of birds long awake. He saw lapwings soaring almost vertically to catch flying insects and high above a majestic eagle circling slowly in a sky so clear and blue. He drew breath at the scent of marsh and pasture that drifted towards him. He never ceased to wonder at the regeneration the seasons were capable of. He smiled to himself as he continued thinking of his sister.

He went to meet her and greeted her shyly, unsure of what to say. He admired the cut of her expensive suit and sensible walking shoes and guided her along the path to the house where they had both been children. They talked easily about their lives and different fortunes, letting the other only glimpse the surface, not the depths. Donald had not talked for such length in decades and was mildly exhilarated at using vocabulary long neglected.

He noticed that time had not been kind to Moira. Her face was drawn and he saw bitterness in her gaunt eyes that did not reflect the dignity and grace of her expensive clothes.

He led her through the door of the house. There was a large bucket of marsh flowers by the fireplace. He had picked them that morning, remembering her love for them. He had rearranged the house so that its comfort would welcome a visitor. Moira looked around and wrinkled her nose in distaste.

"The same old sticks and ugly furniture I see. How can you live with it, Donald?"

His heart sank with disappointment. "It suits me well enough for what I want."

"That is quite evident." She answered harshly. Her own house in a fashionable area of Vancouver was polished and gleaming, expensive and cold. Correct for mid-day bridge with her ladies' committees. A burnished reflection of the constant show to paper over the void of life that she had never lived. Her escape from the poverty of her island life had not provided freedom from her bitterness.

She walked around the room and into the kitchen, inspecting the carpets, chairs and ragged curtains.

"You should get rid of all this. I'll send you what you need from Vancouver. Don't worry, I'll pay. The least I can do for my neglect of you."

Donald was stunned. "Is that all you can see, Moira?" he said gently. "These sticks you despise are just simple parts of what I have here. I'm content with them. If they offend you, look not at them. Did you see the marsh flowers I picked for you this morning? In the bucket there. You used to like them."

She turned and looked at his gesture and felt the sting of his soft rebuke. She bit her lips to control the mounting venom. She thought, how dare he live in this simplicity. Who was he to turn his back on the world and live just as he pleased?

"Why do you stay here, cut off from everything?"

Donald shrugged and gazed out the window, "I don't really know why, it just seemed to happen that way." His gentleness was a spur to Moira's deep well of bitterness.

"I'll tell you why," she snapped. "You're hiding here in this hovel. You could never leave this island because deep down you're a total failure." She paused for breath, "Out there is a world that takes guts and backbone. You - you're spineless." She stopped for a moment at the look of amazement on her brother's face.

"You could have been the best fisherman in these islands, yes and a writer too. But just look at you secluded here with your sheep subsidies and quiet. You would be exposed anywhere else for what you are. A failure. That's what keeps you here on this island." She finished with a sharp edge to her words, intended to cut her brother.

Slowly Donald felt the well of bitterness that his sister drew from. With quiet composure he spoke.

"Moira, if that is so, then why must you come back to reveal this truth to me? Why do you think you have to make sure I understand why I am here?" At her silence he continued. "I'll tell you why. There's a simplicity here that offends you, that reminds you of where you came from, an honesty before God that you fear to recognize. This is a rebuke to the empty round of shallow gatherings you fill your life with. That's why you came back to this island, to fill your emptiness, to scoff at simplicity while you snatch at it for yourself. There's a reminder here, of how poor we were, and why you left only to be scoffed at by those richer than yourself. What you once were and could have been is too much for you to accept. You chose your life, ashamed of us here but you know full well where the balance of truth lies."

The colour mounted on Moira's cheeks as his voice grew more insistent. His strange nobility eased her bitterness and for a moment she relaxed. There was an emotionally charged silence. They faced one another across the kitchen table, the same one they had cracked clams on when they were children. The fury and shock of their words made them tremble. Moira's lips quivered as she choked off a retort of condemnation of how he lived. She turned away from Donald's piercing eyes and words.

He let out a long breath, stepped to Moira's side and put his hand on her arm. "What are we saying to one another Moira? Thirty years and all we do is hurt with words? We've learned very little then. Come and walk to the shore with me and let the autumn breeze take the evil from our tongues."

Donald stopped walking at the shore and turned to his sister,

"There is so much we never spoke of over the years. I know you suffered when we lost our brother John in a car crash."

Moira looked up at her brother with tears in her eyes.

He said, "After John's death you had to leave and I resolved to stay. We dealt with the tragedy in the only ways we could – without understanding one another. We left scars on one another's hearts and never really healed. Now at our age, surely to goodness could we not be gentle and forgiving of one another?"

Moira nodded through her trembling and gladly followed her brother's views. They walked slowly along the shore and Moira surprisingly slipped her hand through his arm as she warmed to him.

Donald pointed out things to her - gently reminding her of what they had come from, easing her mind with stories of the sheep running away with the washing and rabbiting with their brother John. They stood by the shore. Two figures in middle age briefly united in a semblance of peace.

"Well Moira, I may be a bit of a failure in some eyes."

"No, no Donald please let me take back my words I didn't mean to…"

"You can have back the pain, my sister, but not the words. There's some truth in them. But realize that here in a terrible fashion to you and others I at least survive in the shadow of truth and eternity. Derelict and simpleton that I appear, I might just understand a little of the way of things."

They stood in silence for a long time, tired and spent from their emotions. Moira felt an overwhelming relief as Donald walked with her to the road where her car was parked. They were at last comfortable with one another.

They enjoyed an almost private agreement and Moira exulted in her brother's surprising invincibility. She smiled openly to him for the first time, without guile or bitterness tracing her features.

"Thank you Donald and may God's blessings be with you."

"And with you Moira."

She drove away. He knew he would not see her again but rejoiced that they could give God's blessing to one another. Donald glanced at the darkening autumn sky and knew there would soon be a first snow on the northern mountains.

He smiled to himself and returned to his solitude and isolation, relieved once more to shun the company of his fellow humans.

# 8. Thomas's Fantastic Day

Thomas's day started early, just after dawn. He was awakened by something intangible about the morning.

Leaving his snoring brother, Archie, whose bed he shared, he tiptoed past the back room where his older sister, Morag, muttered and turned in her sleep.

Thomas shivered as he pulled on his green sweater and trousers in the cold kitchen. He drank a cup of milk from the pitcher by the scullery and left the cup on the table. His mother would notice and know that he had gone.

He made up the fire and put a match to it to take the chill from the kitchen for the rest of his family. Then, all of eleven years old, he was drawn into his day of adventure.

Closing the door behind him, he stood and marvelled at the beauty of the morning. The aftermath of dawn could be traced in a sky streaked with reds and grays, as though a child had smeared pastels on the horizon.

He walked from his house, skirting the bay that led to the pier. Here and there a light showed from a home, but no one was about. This hour of the morning belonged to Thomas and to the sheep - their dominance uninterrupted by merchants opening up shop. It was too early for children to run to school shouting and laughing, too early for the first drunk to take up their station by the lifeboat shed.

Thomas counted the small boats clustered by the slipway then made his way to the jetty.

Two trawler boats with their crew asleep below lay at anchor in the lee of the breakwater.

The clamour of gulls around them gave vocal testimony to the remains of last night's catch. The boy spat into the water and watched the ever-increasing number of rings on the calm surface.

He spat again, this time to the left so the two sets of rings would collide, fuse and then break on the pier's pilings. Small patches of oil drifted past like multi-coloured jellyfish. In his waiting, he scanned the pier and took in the fishing nets hung on rails and piled in disarray amongst discarded warp lines and fuel drums.

The sea was calm and flat as glass, scarcely responding to the whisper-like breeze that brushed it. Thomas heard the noise of a diesel engine and stared out to sea, straining his attention to catch the shape of the vessel. He knew the sound of it and peered anxiously until he was able to see the familiar outline of his uncle's fishing boat making its way toward the dock. His uncle Michael lived on a neighbouring island, yet came to this pier for fuel.

The boy willed the boat to come faster, before the village stirred, before his sister took him along with herself to school. He had been promised a trip on the boat, and today he wanted to go. He looked anxiously to the village, at the first signs of life there, and at the church clock that showed he would not be spared Morag's insistence.

The wash at the bow of the boat grew bigger as it drew near. The postmaster, filling his pipe before his day of commerce began, saw Thomas and waved. The boy reluctantly acknowledged the salute as his elder brother, Archie, shouted from the hill to get along to school. Then Morag was before him, an amused quietness in her eyes. Reluctantly, Thomas allowed himself to be pulled into the way of things and followed her to school.

Unable to concentrate on his lessons, Thomas stared though the schoolroom window at his uncle's boat at the pier. Then, when his teacher Miss MacDougall turned toward the blackboard, he cautiously moved from desk to desk until he was close to the schoolroom door.

As his classmates giggled quietly, stifling their mirth behind fists over their mouths, Thomas slipped out the door, down the brae, and through the cut to the pier where Michael and Angus were standing, smoking.  The morning sun cast a sheen on the water that was scarcely rippled by the wind coming from the west. Several trawlers had tied up at the pier and their crews were busy taking on ice and sorting their catch for market on the mainland.

Thomas paused at the school gate and as he cast a glance back at the school, he caught Miss MacDougall's smile on him. He stood still, unsure of retreat or flight. He was no stranger to her ruler across his knuckles, yet she was there looking at him and smiling. She turned from the window. He did not understand his teacher, yet exulted in his release, knowing of the punishment awaiting him the next day at school.

He felt his uncle's gaze on him. "You're a wee bugger, Thomas, jumping school the day. What will your teacher do when she gets hold of you, eh?"

"But she saw me and smiled as I took the short-cut to the pier."

While his uncle wondered, old Angus nodded to Thomas to get aboard. Michael and Angus had stopped in their smoking and looked at the boy as he shyly stood before them - a small slip of nothing, elf-like and ephemeral. This was his first time on the boat, and, as it pulled away from the pier, he went out to sea feeling like a bird soaring with wings wide open.

As Angus and Michael talked about where the fleets of creels would be placed, Thomas sat quietly looking at them. Later, he shared their sandwiches over lunch, sipped tea from Angus's large mug and listened to their talk of the sea. They did not explain anything to him. He learned by listening, watching and then doing - resulting in a left hand ugly and red with two large welts suffered from lobster nips. He had borne the pain in silence, but his tears had been noticed by the two men. They treated him with a gentle courtesy, which he shyly treasured.

Angus sat on a wooden fish box filling his pipe. His pale blue eyes were rarely away from the sea that sustained him. His weathered features, broad shoulders and massive hands were a contrast to the eager-faced boy beside him. Michael started the engine and the boat headed to the islands further south to pick up lobster traps. He slowed the vessel as they approached an inlet close to Mieray Island. In the shadows of the soaring cliffs Angus's incantations sung softly under his breath.

"Lobster. No Lobster. No Lobster. Crabs. Lobster. Crabs." Like a medieval incantation old Angus sang out his greeting as the lobster creels came over the gunwale of the boat one by one. "Lobster. No Lobster. Crab." Uttered with same pitch and feeling, he intoned a greeting to the creature trapped within. His huge hands deftly unlaced the latticed side of the creel, and, with a slow rhythm, he methodically passed the lobsters to Thomas who transferred them to a large wooden box covered with a wet sack. He watched in fascination as Angus tore claws, shell and legs from the living crab to place the breast meat in the creel as bait, along with a salt mackerel.

When the whole fleet of twenty creels was stacked on the deck, Michael shouted above the noise of the engine to Angus that they were moving. If the old man heard he did not acknowledge but peered keenly at the sea as the

Atlantic swell rocked the boat in its turning. Angus was well attuned to the many moods of the Ocean. With a short, slow movement of his hand, he directed the skipper to move closer to a reef. Then once the spot was chosen, Angus again motioned to Michael to motor in a large semicircle as he cast the baited creels back into the sea.

Angus had fished these waters for forty years and was still awed by nature's stark edifice. Climbing sheer from the sea to nine hundred feet, the cliffs drew their eyes. It was as if to redefine their apartness that a fleet of creels was set in a channel that cut through the soaring grandeur of the cliffs. An act of impudence to snatch a morsel from the feet of the gods, the boat slowly picked its way through the dark channel. Angus deposited the baited creels into the sea, taking bearings from rocks he had brushed against countless times. All three blinked as they emerged from the grotto and sunlight brought them back to the day. Angus and Thomas busied themselves with securing the catch in wooden boxes that would be floated at a mooring in their home bay. The boy's arms and back ached from the lifting of heavy creels and his left hand throbbed painfully. Angus observed this and put Thomas in the wheelhouse with Michael.

The noise of the engine made conversation impossible yet Michael shouted volubly above the roar. Thomas still could not hear. His replies were similarly incomprehensible. They enjoyed their mutually unintelligible conversation all the way back to the pier. The osmosis of the sea and beauty of the day united them in a way that required no words.

Thomas was dispatched home with a large bag of crab claws, and Michael and Angus took on fuel drums for the boat as he walked along the pier road and up the hill. He moved the bag of crab claws from arm to arm as its weight strained his small, tired muscles. His sister met him at the rise of the brae and helped to carry the bag. Her bright red skirt was a counterpoint to Thomas's green sweater. He stopped at the top of the brae and waved with happiness as Michael and Angus returned to their island.

It was now dark and Thomas told the story of his day to his family while the crab claws cooked and split in the embers of the fire. He sat at the large kitchen table with small flecks of crab meat on his chin. His sister Morag demanded repeated telling of his day off from school. At one point she seized her brother and waltzed him around the kitchen until they collided with their mother and tumbled to the floor, all legs, arms and merriment. Maggie, their mother, laughed with her son and daughter, delighted at Thomas's adventure.

"If you're for dancing the pair o' ye, we'll have it done differently. Archie, fetch your accordion."

Archie had watched his brother and sister whirl round the kitchen floor with admiration and not a little envy. He was not given easily to joy, too stolid for one on the verge of adulthood, but his transformation lay in music. With delicate rhythms and chords his fingers brought forth music from the accordion. He directed the energetic scramble of his kin to slow strathspeys, then vigorous reels. When at last the two were intoxicated by their steps, they danced solo opposite one another, fiercely competitive now, turning and twisting with the grace of gulls. Thomas was almost as light of step as his sister Morag, but her grace was something not of this world. At last Archie released them from his music. He was now part of them and could join in their animation.

Maggie wove the web of riddles and conversation that tied her offspring to her, feeding them, humoring them. The door opened to admit Bernard, the old widower from the next house, who called nightly to fetch a jug of milk.

He knew of Thomas's adventure and stumped into the kitchen with a mock fierceness, demanding that the boy give a full account of himself. With a grin Thomas started on the retelling and soon old Bernard was chuckling and slapping his thigh. The retelling was done several times more that evening as other neighbours, drawn by the music, came in, listened to the boy, feasted on crabs and drank from the bottle of whiskey that had appeared. The large kitchen table was pushed back to make room for the company to wend its way through a reel. Morag was called to dance and Archie's music drew forth delicate, poignant steps from her.

Bernard, the widower, cleared his throat and began to recite a poem. It was received with murmurs of approval as he gave the story of the transportation of Highlanders from their hills and crofts across oceans and ice-laden waters to Canada, where a living was now carved out of the wilderness. He told of their heartbreak at being torn from their nurturing. His epic was received in a silence that was too eloquent. After a long pull at the bottle of whisky, old Bernard struck up a ribald song about the adventures of a cockerel and the company learned to laugh again. Soon however, the songs and Archie's music were lost to the young boy. He lay fast asleep by the hearth, his small body curled to catch the warmth of the fire's dying embers. Around him conversation had turned to crops, the sea, the latest catches by the fishermen, but he was oblivious to it all. Archie gently picked up his sleeping brother and carried him to his bed, unlacing the boy's shoes and drawing off his trousers.

"Good night to you Thomas, my brave lad."

Then Archie returned to the company, the conversation and gossip that were a prelude to the evening's end. And Thomas slept.

# 9: Earth Burning

My grandnephew, Christopher, was celebrating his birthday. He told me he felt awful about being nine years old and wished he could stay five years old forever. When I asked him why, he replied that if he could stay five, then the Earth would not explode into flames. His lips quivered and tears welled in his large brown eyes.

"I am scared it is too late, that there will be nothing to save," he exclaimed with a frightened voice. He dropped the unopened gift in his hand. I gently guided him from the hallway of his home to sit with me on the garden steps in the back yard where it was quiet.

He said, "I don't want to grow up and live in a world that is burning."

A long silence stretched between us. I could not say that everything will be okay. He was too intelligent for such placebos. So, I spoke to him about the mindfulness community I have created and the steps we have taken for planetary care. We simplify, make do with less, share and adapt. An important part of our intent is to create environmental leaders and that includes him.

"Why not become a leader for your generation?" I asked him. He thought about that and asked what else the community did.

I pointed out that we encourage voluntary simplicity and community ethics as a way of life. We start with the Earth. Our large organic garden produces an abundance of vegetables, apples and flowers that are shared with neighbors and community members.

It is a solace for me to spend time with the Earth, observing bumblebees and butterflies while gardening with assistance from neighborhood children. I told him that the kids laughed hilariously when they saw that the vegetable plant I had carefully nurtured for months turned out to be a giant weed - not a tomato plant!

At the back of the garden, next to the tall cedar hedge, is a beautiful fountain that murmurs to the abundant flowers, which find their way to the elderly folk living on our crescent. A solar panel on the roof fuels the hot water system of our home. Everything else is as eco-friendly as we can make it for our fifty-year-old bungalow with a meditation hall in the basement. This eco-effort has become an example for many friends. They consider how much we are saving and implement something similar.

Our focus is on mindfulness in schools and city environment, teens at risk and the empowerment of women. I admitted to Christopher that I was amazed by the results. At the local level there were great women who helped make things happen.

"You mean girl power?" he asked incredulously.

"Exactly that," I replied "I believe that the present millennium  is the century of the daughters, not so much as a gender separation thing, but as attributes of a holistic, nurturing presence of mind."

I told Christopher that the idea is to foster a strong group of people in Ottawa to make a difference for the betterment of society and the Earth. Women are in the forefront of this endeavour. I explained that they are the heart that holds the living waters, the dynamic epicentre that leads to effective action. Creating a different course of action and living is how we will get things done. Christopher understood my poetic reference.

He was taking it all in. I suggested that when enough of us change, then our ideas will be in charge. I told him about a speech I had given at Ottawa City Hall about the consequences of pathological consumption. It pointed out that festive occasions like Christmas provide opportunities for the best and the worst within us to come out and play. Although compassion and kindness are there, they are often swamped by greed, selfishness and consumer madness. We need to re-assess, to move on from being self-absorbed, greedy and distracted.

"How?" Christopher asked again. He really wanted to know.

I chose my words carefully.

"We must locate in something bigger than ourselves: a humanitarian cause, respecting the earth, making our thinking better, being kinder and more generous. How about examining our habits about gift giving and learn to give in a different way? You know what, Christopher, I no longer buy Christmas gifts, instead I present gift certificates such as education for a girl in Afghanistan, micro-loans for female led families, rebuilding forests in Haiti, literacy packages and mosquito nets where needed. Such gifts are bigger than ourselves and create happiness for less fortunate people."

I told him how my grandchildren proudly take their Christmas certificates to school and play it forward with their class and teachers. One boy on the crescent where I live in Ottawa has received such gifts from me for several years. For his recent birthday, he asked his friends not to give presents, but to bring a donation for the Ottawa Humane Society that looks after hurt animals. All of his friends brought donations, a splendid sum of two hundred and eighty dollars. They went together to the Humane Society and happily handed their bag of cash to the surprised staff. Other children in the neighborhood have followed suit.

This resonated with Christopher. He said, "I can do something like that with my ice hockey team. My dad is the coach, and he would help." He waited for me to continue.

"The greatest gift we can give to ourselves and others at this time is sharing and caring. It involves stepping onto what the Buddhists call the Bodhisattva Path." (Christopher knows that I am a Zen teacher). I explained that a Bodhisattva is a person who stays in the global mess and does their best to awaken the minds and hearts of people. I firmly stated that it is time for the Bodhisattva-within-us to enter the twenty-first century as the example for action. It takes training, practice, intelligence and creative vision.

"You mean like Jedi training?" he enquired.

I nodded with a smile and referred briefly to my years of training in ashrams and monasteries in India and France, though confided that the real kicker for me was the time spent with indigenous medicine people in the Canadian wilderness.

I knew that his greatest fear was about the planet's ecological crises. He worried about mining disasters in Brazil and China, wildfires in Canada's Boreal forests and Amazon deforestation. I affirmed that he was correct about his worries. I asked him to listen carefully to me.

"Let's face it, Christopher, our industrial civilization is a system devouring itself, dislocating the organic structures of the Earth to the point that all species, not just our own, are at risk. It has taken us to a dangerous precipice. From there we stare into the abyss of climate emergency, ecosystem collapse, resource wars, terrorism, permanent refugees and anarchy. Are we at an end game without a philosophy for the future?" He was very intelligent and grasped this high level conversation.

Before giving him a few more scenarios I did slow walking meditation around the back garden, focusing on what I would say. I stopped for a moment at the running fountain with hollyhocks on one side and roses on the other. Then came back to the steps where he was sitting.

"The UN reported that in 1990 more than 20 billion metric tons of carbon dioxide was placed in the atmosphere from fossil fuels. By 2018, it was in excess of 32.5 billion metric tons, accompanied by the deadly tsunamis, earthquakes, tornadoes, wildfires, sea level inundations destroying low lying coastal regions of the planet."

He was taken aback by my opening words.

"Professor James Anderson at Harvard University asserts that due to the present warming in oceans the amount of water vapor now in the atmosphere triggers storm systems that are violent to the extreme. The West Antarctic Ice Sheet is now melting ten times faster than average. As it weakens, rising sea levels of several meters are to be expected. The knock-on consequences create more destructive cyclones, tsunamis and tornadoes that will destroy human habitation along with other species."

I sat down on the steps next to him, then asked him to walk around the garden with me. We then sat on the green painted bench next to the fountain. There was a long silence.

He then asked, "So, how do we reverse the destruction of the planet?"

I waited a while, to carefully lay out the situation, "We must come to a stop, locate ourselves in stillness, and make different choices by examining our minds and patterns of consumption. We must look at how we actually participate in creating these terrible disasters. This kind of awareness takes us back to what we do with our minds."

"Just how?" was his one-line mantra.

I shocked him by saying, "You can start by making friends with your breath," Christopher looked up at me quizzically.

"Bring your focus and attention to your inhale as it comes in, then on your exhale as it goes out. Really concentrate on the whole length of breath coming in and breath going out. Do this ten times. This kind of focus peels away anxiety, frustration and anger so that you become calm and clear. Try it with me and notice the difference for yourself."

He did so and grinned. I told Christopher that we do know how to reduce our ecological footprint. We also know that taking care of the Earth is also taking care of ourselves. We must begin it now for the future. Our tomorrow is shaped by the actions we take right now. I suggested to Christopher that was enough for him to digest, but he insisted, "No, I want to hear more. Tell me about the big deal about your speech on pathological consumption."

I could not turn away from his intelligent eagerness. I replied that mindless consumption totally dominates our planet, mind and body. I mentioned that if rampant consumption remains our deepest desire we will continue to degrade the planet, eventually destroying its ability to harbor life. His fears were correct. I stood up and picked up a broom to brush away some leaves that had fallen on the paths. Then I went on to say,

"Valentine's Day, Easter, Christmas, Mother's Day and so on are targeted by the captains of industry for optimal retail returns, and mindless consumerism is fuelled to the max. At Christmas we are often far removed from remembering the significance of this spiritual celebration. Our current unsustainable energy and economic systems are subsystems of a global ecology that is disintegrating before our very eyes. We must simplify, make do with less and change, or the burning world will definitely occur."

I continued, "Did you know that we also harm our bodies through the food we eat, and that it has disastrous consequences for our connection to all living beings?"

He did not, yet his intelligent mind was a sponge soaking up every word.

"The vast consumption of meat and alcohol creates an excessive ecological footprint. Industrial animal agriculture is not really farming. Animals are treated solely as economic commodities and subjected to horrible cruelty. The stress, despair and anger generated in the animals are the energies we consume when they end up on our plate."

"That is so gross," he remarked.

I told Christopher that we can change our minds and patterns of food consumption. We re-educate and retrain ourselves through meditation and choosing to support our body and planet by shifting ingrained habits. It takes training, but we can begin to step more lightly on the planet. It means reducing as much as possible the violence, destruction and suffering brought to living creatures and to the planet. Bringing peace into our own biological system and consciousness, inevitably brings it to all the other systems that we engage with through our thoughts, speech and actions.

"Is this your Buddhism?" he asked.

I smiled before speaking, "The Buddha was very smart. He taught that the world is always burning, but burning with the fires of greed, anger and foolishness. His advice was simple - drop such dangers as soon as possible. The Buddha taught that it was unskillful speech, selfish feelings, negative mental formations, wrong perceptions and badass consciousness that burned the world."

Christopher asked, "Did the Buddha really use the term badass?"

I said, "The Buddha did not say "badass" - that was my embellishment."

Then I pointed out that the Hopi people also referred to the burning as a state of imbalance known as *Koyaanisqatsi*. We are not the first generation to experience this. The difference today is that without our commitment to wise intervention about climate change, we could be the last.

"Is climate change our basic problem then?" he asked.

I paused for a moment before replying. "The basic issue is whether we can adapt to climate change. Remember when we talked about the 2015 Paris Accord on Climate Change?"

He nodded.

"It was certainly an exceptional step by the international community, showing their determination to prevent global temperatures from rising a further 1.5 degrees. What was missing from all the deliberations and press releases was a candid recognition of the "Cascade Effect," a notion from ecological science. Tipping points in sea level rise and temperature connect to tipping points in air pollution, which connect to tipping points in polar ice melt, hurricanes and forest wildfires. All of these triggers create further tipping points that create deforestation, floods, desertification and so on in a relentless cascade."

I reminded him of the wildfires in British Columbia and California, pointing out that the entire boreal forest in Canada is a tinder box due to climate change. He understood the reality that it is not about a reversal of climate change but about learning how to adapt to the *consequences* of climate change. I emphasized to him that the disasters all over the world interconnect. Whether it is wildfires, floods, landslides, volcanic eruptions, hurricanes, tsunamis or millions of aquatic creatures dead on beaches - it is all connected. The media and news reporters often cast science to the wind when they report the drama and hype of terrible things happening worldwide. They rarely tell the truth that this is another manifestation of climate change. Certain news programs promote corporate interests that contribute to these interconnected disasters. The general public is not educated by the media about the terrible disasters happening on our planet. The other obstacles that prevent the general public from taking wise action are a mixture of fear, despair, laziness, disempowerment and a sense of hopelessness.

I then looked at Christopher, "Maybe this is why you want to stay five years old forever. The difficult thing for you, for anyone, to grasp is that we are the primary cause. People *are* aware, but just feel helpless in the face of climate change. So what are we to do?"

He shrugged in exasperation.

"Here's the thing," I said. "In terms of action, we have clear data-based evidence that we must cut back, make do with less, and implement a lifestyle of voluntary simplicity. So, where do we start? Of course we must think globally and be aware of the bigger picture despite fear and disempowerment. But we can also act locally in our families and communities. Our intentions then spread like ripples from a pebble dropped in still water. We can hold officials, politicians and corporate culture accountable. We can tell the politicians and corporate decision makers that we, as voters and consumers, are deeply concerned about the planet and our impact on it."

I continued speaking on a personal note,

"Christopher, the challenge for me is to be *in* society, but as a still island of mindfulness. Take small steps at first, then larger ones. We just need to make essential changes in energy use, diet, language, media and outreach. Voluntary simplicity is a good starting place. It means making deliberate choices about how we spend time and money. We can support environmental causes with the excess clutter in the basement and always think about whether we really "need" to buy something more. Enjoy being simple and living modestly by shifting our perceptions just a little bit. If we look deeply into what we do with time, money, clutter and our choices, then we can change. Notice whether the consequences are peace and happiness for you. To avoid drastic outcomes, it is wise to take training very seriously. This helps to avoid all the negative stuff I have told you about."

"Wow," exclaimed Christopher. "Okay, I get it about training, but what does that look like?" I was relieved by his intelligent question but hesitant to talk to him about what I was thinking. He was watching me closely and said, "Just lay it out for me."

I then proceeded to talk about "Gardening in the Mind" - a basic Buddhist strategy. I offered him eight simple steps to refine the mind and then engage differently with the world.

Learn to be silent and quiet. Clear time and space for spiritual practice at home and throughout your daily schedule.

Create a stress reduction menu and subtract the "weeds" - the negative energies - in the garden of your mind.

Be determined to meditate daily to do the weeding.

Focus on and soften your heart. Do not be mean - cultivate the soil of your mind's garden.

Cultivate the seeds of mindfulness - love, compassion, joy, equanimity - and promote them at home, school, work or in solitude.

Simplify, make do with less, declutter your mind and home.

Become aware of how your spiritual practice changes your mind.

The outcome is that you can better engage with the world.

Christopher was entering all of this on his tablet as I continued to talk.

"Our ways of living together, caring for environmental, political and economic realms need to be reconstructed. Gardening in the Mind has the capacity to transform how we think and how to cultivate mindfulness. Finding stillness and inner silence is a necessary first step. We have to find a way to create the conditions for this to happen. In our modern world of fast-paced lifestyles, there are so many distractions that make us outwardly dependant and un-centered. We also find it easier to close rather than open our hearts. But the remedy is within reach. We can unravel the knots of suffering and move from being mindless to being mindful. This is achieved by gardening in the mind. The eight point menu helps."

I paused for a while to find the words to bring my conversation with Christopher to an end. "Christopher, why do you think we should do this stuff?"

He shrugged.

"Here's why. When you are open and receptive, you become an inspiration for others. Also, when you can learn to be with pain, face-to-face with what hurts, breathing in and out, you feel the sting recede as you calm. If you start to close down, just ask yourself, "Do I really want to take a pass on happiness?" Remember this - always let go once you feel you are closing down or clinging."

Then I surprised him,

"I have a fridge magnet at home with the words LET GO OR BE DRAGGED. I see it every day, and I take that message to heart. It is essential to learn to be silent, to stop clinging, and to find the way to be present in the moment. As the Hopi advise us, never take anything personally and look around to see who is with you. Doing these things helps the world to change. Such a destination is well worth your effort don't you think?"

He grinned and nodded in agreement. I assured Christopher that we are equal to the task, and I chose not to hold back anything from him during this long conversation on his birthday. He is an unusually bright boy, as he asked questions and demanded clarification. Yet I knew he had grasped what I had said.

He came up to me as I was leaving and whispered in my ear that my chat with him was his best birthday present ever.

# 10: Torched

She recognized the lengthy gait of the man walking toward her on the beach.

"Simon, what are you doing?" she exclaimed.

He snapped round, trying to hide the petrol can in his hand. Sweat beaded on his face and stained the armpits of his shirt.

He muttered a curse and shouted angrily, "It's none of your fucking business. Get away from me." His face twisted with anger.

She pointed to the petrol can.

He trembled, all six feet of him, in fear of the determined young woman who had caught him. His jeans and work boots had splashes of petrol on them and his dark eyes searched desperately around to see if anyone else had seen him.

"I have to set the house up there ablaze. The owner has not paid his dues to the land owner." Then with a touch of shame, "It's my job to do this. There is nothing else for me in this god forsaken place."

"You will not torch the old man's house."

Simon breathed heavily several times before replying, "If I do not, you know that it will be me that gets torched. That's how it works."

The silence was vibrant with anger, fear and shame. At last she spoke, "How far you have fallen, Simon. You need help."

He stepped towards her, desperate to remember better times and snarled, "How can you help me then?"

She took the petrol can from his hand and calmly spoke, "The old man has been moved to an institution in the city and will not return."

He then gasped as he saw her unscrew the can and splash the petrol over the wooden door and windows of the small house. She struck a match and threw it on the petrol soaked door.

As she passed the empty petrol can to her eldest brother, the blaze lit the somber evening on the beach. She relaxed and said to him, "Your task is completed and nobody died. It is time you left this place for good."

Simon grimly nodded his head. "I think you are correct."

# 11. Science, Climate Change, Global Pandemic

Many years ago, (2008), I published *Failsafe: Saving the Earth from Ourselves*. I wrote about homo sapiens as perhaps a failed genetic experiment.

I delivered the content of this book to students at Carleton University in a television course I created on "Ecology and Culture."

Halfway through the course I looked out at the young people and offered an apology – that my generation had not left a healthy planet for them.

Much later in 2019, I participated in the climate strikes on Parliament Hill in Ottawa. I recalled that apology when surrounded by thousands of magnificent children. It was quite emotional for me to hear them shouting out for politicians to get behind the science. I was in admiration of their strike, yet sad that Earth matters had not changed for the better. I noticed that I was not the only grandparent who cried a bit.

However, a brilliant pushback to climate denial had been made by Polly Higgins, a fellow Scot. She was a barrister and created a world-wide campaign to criminalize *ecocide*; the name given to describe the destruction of ecosystems by the carbon cabal and their political lackeys.

The legal instrument of ecocide has been promoted by President Macron of France and the European Union.

Polly Higgins' idea has garnered worldwide momentum to hold corporate executives and governments liable for the damage they do to ecosystems and humanity.

The legal work demanded specific legal changes to protect the earth for future generations of all species. Unfortunately, Polly Higgins died from cancer on Easter Day, April 21, 2019. Her strong belief was that such a law would change the world. Her work continues with a vast legal team in many countries. Her everlasting quip will never be forgotten: "I have a choice to protect our Earth, or let it be destroyed." These are the stakes we all face.

The campaign of criminalizing ecocide is growing. The Marshall Islands and Maldives in the Pacific Ocean have brought legal requests to the UN about their dire situation with rising sea levels, to make ecocide a criminal act in order to curb the damage done by corporations. Global lawyers are working to make ecocide an international crime at the International Criminal Court. International jurist and human rights expert, Valerie Cabanes, has this to say,

"The current climate and ecological disruptions are fuelling injustice and geopolitical tensions while those ransacking the planet go unpunished. It is therefore urgent to demand new forms of responsibility and solidarity, by recognizing a fifth international crime, the "crime of ecocide."

We've had the scientific knowledge since 1980 to create the solution to Climate Emergency, but the obstacles were not technical or scientific. They were the attitudes, values and concepts that define the dominance of corporate values - and their bottom line of profits was upheld by successive governments that devalued science. It was never about science. It was about the brand of economics favoured by Big Oil and other multi-national corporations promoting carbon extraction, irrespective of the damage caused to ecosystems and populations. Their collusion suppressed science, confused public knowledge with misinformation, and beefed up the blatant bribery of politicians.

Did anyone notice that degradation of the Earth's ecology was the catalyst for radical Climate Change? Food crops were destroyed by horrendous heat waves as carbon dioxide poured into the atmosphere. Did no one realize that food riots and world panic trace back to one cause – the economic agenda of corporations? The undercover deal between governments and multi-nationals was invested in political and economic structures that centered on the carbon combustion complex. This collective agenda destabilized world order and endangered the world's populations. Billionaire backers protected their profits, downplayed scientific conclusions, and deliberately dulled the intelligence of the general public. They paid selected scientists to promote the position that the existing evidence on climate change does not support crisis warnings. This is a bought and sold lie! Everyone knew the lack of truth – the US government, corporations, and industrialists – all knew the truth. To keep the bottom line of profits in their favour, they were willing to accept that civilization would be destroyed in the not-so-distant future.

December 2020 signified the fifth anniversary of the Paris Climate Agreement. The UN Secretary General addressed 70 heads of states and governments. He warned that every country must declare again for an immediate climate emergency, as real progress had not been made to make the Paris agreement a reality. Antonio Guterres, the UN Secretary General, criticized rich countries for not spending the $100billion  a year that had been promised. It did not happen, as climate warming since 2015 had been the warmest on record.

From global health, pandemic, climate emergency to racial injustice – 2020 severely tested humanity's resilience. The brilliant indigenous response from Robin Wall Kimmerer's *Braiding Sweetgrass: Indigenous Wisdom, Scientific Knowledge and the Teachings of Plants* (2020), is very clear: "What was needed was the wisdom of environmental science, the clarity of philosophical analysis and the creative power of the written word, to find new ways to understand and reimagine our relation to the natural world. We seem to be living in an era of economics of fabricated demand and compulsive overconsumption… we continue to embrace economic systems that prescribe infinite growth on a finite planet… we need reforms that would ground economics in ecological principles and the constraints of thermodynamics. Climate change will unequivocally defeat economics that are based on constant taking without giving in return."

Dave Courchene is the founder of Turtle Lodge International Centre for Indigenous Education and Wellness. He and his council across Canada provide wisdom teachings for the world. They see COVID-19 as a symptom of an exhausted planet that requires a healthy relationship between humanity and Mother Earth. Their main concern is the disastrous disconnect of humankind from the land and its lessons. The planet needs not only a cure for COVID-19 - it also requires a cure for humanity's reliance on multi-national greed.

The COVID–19 pandemic is killing people world-wide. It is necessary to follow the science, and to put into place the Indigenous view of living on this planet. Otherwise, our future will be to face disaster in both spheres of science.

The coronavirus pandemic has devastated our planet. Health officials appear every day on TV news providing protocols such as social distancing, wearing masks, hand washing and reducing contacts.

However, the health officials' directions were often ignored by considerable populations who insist on their freedom to do whatever they wish, particularly with the economy. The balance between government and population was often seen by them as oppressive.

Scientists do not yet know the full nature of the virus – its effects on the body and just how lethal it can be to different populations. Any nation decimated by such a disease cannot expect to have a functioning economy, partly due to the damage that occurs to both mental and physical health.

Science has been racing to create workable vaccines. Vaccines usually require years of research and testing, yet in 2020 scientists embarked in record time to create safe and effective coronavirus vaccines.

Phase 1 trials involve testing in a small group to see if it is safe and effective. Phase 2 involves a larger group and various potential doses. Phase 3 trials are a final stage before getting approval – safety, efficacy and optimal dosing all scheduled to involve 30,000 people. There is good news. In the early months of the pandemic Pfizer and BioNTech developed a coronavirus vaccine, claiming that it was 94 per cent effective. They quickly received U.S. Food and Drug Administration approval for use.

However, Pfizer's vaccine requires extreme-cold storage, as it needs to be kept at minus 70 degrees Celsius (-94F). It is based on synthetic mRNA to activate the immune system which requires the frigid cold storage. This cold chain makes delivery somewhat challenging, although governments were quick to provide deep cold storage.

Other vaccines have Phase 3 studies by a number of companies. Moderna Inc, a biotech company, was the second to report vaccine trial results with 30,000 volunteers. It claimed that its vaccine was 94.5% effective in preventing the COVID disease. Moderna had an advantage over Pfizer, as it requires minus 4 degrees F and is safe in conventional freezers. The early vaccines included the Astra Zeneca/Oxford company. They were right behind and their vaccine had an effective, strong immune response, particularly for older individuals.

Novavax, based in Maryland, were also in the early race. At the same time there was a roll out in India of the COVISHIELD vaccine from manufacturers in Pune, India. They had partnered with US based Novavax. With these early results, eleven COVID-19 vaccines were tested in large-scale Phase 3 trials around the world. There were 260 COVID vaccine candidates tracked by the London School of Hygiene and Tropical Medicine.

In the US, Dr. Anthony Fauci, the nation's top infectious disease expert, stressed that the upcoming COVID-19 vaccines are safe and effective. He added that African-American scientists had a strong part in developing the vaccines, particularly Dr. Kizzmekia Corbett, a senior research fellow working with the Vaccine Research Center. She was at the forefront of the development of the vaccine created by Moderna.

Dr. Fauci was acutely aware that many Black and Latino Americans were hesitant to take the vaccine, having felt systemic racism that damaged them.

These announcements offered much needed hope and provided some light at the end of the tunnel. There can be no returning to before until COVID-19 vaccines are made widely available to the world's population. It may take some years for normal life to resume.

Thankfully, the World Health Organization (WHO) provided a platform (COVAX) to support a wide range of COVID-19 vaccines as a lifeline to all corners of the world. Without it the majority of people in the world will be unprotected against the COVID-19 pandemic in all its variants.

The WHO stated that over 80 higher-income economies have confirmed their willingness to participate with COVAX. The USA was not on board given Trump's withdrawal from the WHO.

There were 92 middle and lower-income countries that cannot pay for vaccines. That is where the arm of COVAX came in. It raised over US$700 million and reached a target of US$2 billion in order to provide the vaccines required by poor countries.

COVAX was co-ordinated by GAVI, the Vaccine Alliance, India's Serum Institute and other organizations. They should be able to maximise both the development of vaccines and their delivery to vulnerable populations. The hope is that this would allow COVAX to successfully develop vaccines and get past the inability to pay by poor countries.

Emily Rauhala of the Washington Post, December 18, 2020 writes, "A multilateral effort to develop and distribute vaccines has secured almost 2 billion doses ….. allowing some vulnerable groups in particular countries to get vaccinated in the first part of 2021." She finishes her post with questions about funding and supply for poor countries.

She notes, " …COVAX is one of the only ways that low-income countries will be able to source vaccines" ….. and that "Hoarding by rich countries will leave much of the world without an adequate vaccine supply."

However, the new President in America is following the science – Joe Biden has organized a new COVID Task Force as his first presidential task. There is hope.

# 12: Childhood Bedrooms

Andrei asked her a surprising question, "When you were a child what was your bedroom like?"

Katerina smiled as fond recollections arose in her mind. "I had the most marvelous bedroom. It was more of a music room than a bedroom, full of musical instruments."

She laughed, "I had all these stuffed animals and would place them next to my musical instruments and move them around. My father was such a goof. He would knock on the door and ask if he was to be Elephant, Tinker Bell or Bear and then come in and play their instruments." Andrei rolled with laughter as she continued. "My bedroom had a large bay window and my father would sit there with whatever stuffed animal I assigned to him. Often my mother would come in and conduct the entire ensemble."

Katerina's face lit up with the memories, and she turned to him, "What about you Andrei?"

He pondered whether to reveal too much, then decided to tell her.

"As a child, my bedroom was my sanctuary. My parents were often under police scrutiny for their beliefs. To compensate, they created a safe haven for me." He slowly gathered himself, "In one corner there were books, paintings and wooden stools piled in disarray. My bed had two levels, one for me to sleep upon and the other for my stuffed animals to talk to before sleeping. It was a comfortable bed with large pillows and green checkered blankets. I had a telescope next to the window, and, in my imagination, I would fly to galaxies with my favorite animals."

After a long pause, he said, "Perhaps it was too much of a sanctuary, as I did not like to leave that house, though I had to when my parents entered the Space Agency in Moscow. I did not want to leave my safe bedroom behind, but my father was very smart. He cleared it out and painted it in colors I hated. I begged him and my mother to let me see it one last time."

There was a tremor of emotion in Andrei's voice. Katerina stayed very still.

"On that last visit, mother pointed to the empty window where my telescope once focused on the sky and I felt the loss."

I still remember her saying, "There is nothing to hold you back, Andrei. Your dream is still inside now step into freedom."

"Mother smiled as I looked for the telescope. Nothing was there. My treasures had been boxed and sent on to Moscow."

Andrei then said, "That was how they moved me on from fear rather than have me cling to childhood safety. My mother held my hand, and I stared at the spot where my telescope used to stand."

Katerina reached over and gently closed her hands around his, "And here you are Andrei. I will hold you steady. For always."

He looked at her, raised her hand to his lips, and gently kissed her fingers.

# 13: Respecting Indigenous Wisdom

**Yellow Canoe Red Canoe**

You are here Ancient Wisdom,
shimmering embrace of the river
beckoning my heartbeat.
Speaking to each drop of sweat
that runs from my brow,
as we paddle away from the city.
Ottawa River – home to First Nations,
your spirit throbs in the echo
gently heard until your insistence is everywhere,
Ancient Wisdom.

Sunlight through trees dance on last year's leaves
by the river's edge.
The song of an inside sun seeking infinity.
Voices carry as we struggle upstream
against the current, into the wind.
The mighty river spoke to the forest,
female sources creating intergenerational wisdom
that we hardly touch and rarely heed.

I listen deeply,
willing to step across the divide of regret.
Breaking into the tedium of unused muscles,
leaving behind outmoded views.

The river held the threads of before,
those resolute relationships
accrued over centuries,
that keep Earth beliefs alive.
Then at last, once presence is felt,
this river becomes our rhythm.

Two canoes
- one yellow
- one red
take to the majesty of Ancient Wisdom.
Before the forests were fouled and burned.
Before the wind went mad
and the river died.
Before the air was contaminated
with insane entropy.

Two canoes
- one yellow
- one red.
Speaking of form and grace,
a complement of moving energy,
balancing discord with their song
of different voices:
First taste
Wild One
Ancient One.

## *Past, Present, Future* / Dr. Ian Prattis

Yellow canoe, female, sentient being,
brings the lore of First Nations.
We count coups with this river.
It twists and turns
and forces us into her power.
We feel it with our limbs, minds and bodies
and know her depth of knowing.

Pacing rapids, knee deep in the river's grip,
the water pulls and threatens
our yellow canoe.
Asserting dominion
is the way of the river running through Mother Earth.

Weakened by portages,
cut and scratched by thorns, burnt by sun.
Shoulders aching, back burning
from the ascent of rapids,
searching deep for strength.
Then the wondrous peace of waiting in silence
by river's edge.
Taking the moment to flow
with this river as she speaks quietly
to yellow canoe
Of wavelets losing themselves
and dying on a gently shelving beach.
Birds in song herald our presence,
bold in their inspection of yellow canoe.

## Rain, Storm and Sake

Grey rain, storm-laden day.
Wind and rain lash the shore line edge
restrained by marsh reeds.
Rain falls in dense sheets of water
to separate then dance on the river.
Reminders of our mortality
straining into the wind,
finding the lee in the storm by current's edge
close to the river bank.
Weary from the undiminished rain,
while a storm whipped the river to a fury
where moments before
we had plowed with prevailing winds.

A new wind from the North.
Suddenly hurricane force
biting hard, hurling violence
shaking our bones with its power.
The elements took over minds sinking deeper
As we took shelter and stood
drenched
watching
fearing,
tired to the point of sleeping while standing.

*Past, Present, Future* / Dr. Ian Prattis

I laughed,

as we heated sake to warm ourselves,

taking shelter from the elements' teeth
that had bitten deep into us.
Slurping the sake
filled the silence in the storm,
almost a mere breeze in an empty forest.


We sought the fiery presence of the sun,
hiding behind dark grey expanse.
The heavens opened
and the sun came through, the water calmed.
We noted the river's mood
through the sun's brilliance in its setting,
sinking slowly, luring us to its magnificence
accompanied by a mustering of storm clouds.


A mere respite before fury struck
again,
again and again at our small tents
exposed on a spur of sunset.
The storm forced us to retreat
to a safer, less exposed haven.
Still I could smile and hear
the storm's muted whisper deflected through pine trees.
Listening and feeling your presence
Ancient Wisdom.

## Solitudes

Solitude and silence

run fierce and wild within the river.

Yet it beckons,

placing tendrils deep within

to hook an unknown resolve.

She cries out—

Come to this solitude,

to the silence within.

Our canoes

one yellow

one red

draw close to this silence

eager to taste it.

Frozen, bitter cold in this luring.

The feeling of fingers disappear

in the numbness

cascading from the paddle.

Still the river beckons,

silence and solitude has insistence.

My body tells me

its limits are reached and speaks,

telling me more:

Go through limits

of hesitation and hardship

to the unknown, wherein other parts of self

deeply hidden

may be revealed in crossing boundaries.


May I be protected

in the shelter of your song—

Ancient Wisdom's many voices.

In softness the evening seduces

the day's weariness.

The gift of each day arrives with evening wind,

a momentary stillness

before snow settles on the campfire

and the wind's fury

hurls us away.

The torrents of time.


Each day, before the elements reveal their majesty,

there is a gift from nature

brought by the wind

crashing into our senses.

We recognize storm, snow, wind and torrents

as gifts granted to our opening experience to wonder.

## Snow at Calling-Goose Marsh

Snow dusts our tents

white upon orange,

upon green

reflecting the fire's dying embers

glowing charcoal red.

Placed on a point in Quebec

we listen to the rattle of box cars

behind the CN train,

snaking past on the south shore

travelling west more quickly than we

one yellow canoe

one red

Geese call softly,

settling into the marsh

upstream from our camp.

They call softly before dawn when we awake

to the beginning day

with frozen hands, frosted breath

warm fire and quick breakfast.

Even silence is frozen.

Then in one synchronized moment

the geese rise massively

in freezing wind,

brushing past the poplars

that guard our canoes.


Steadily, slowly the camp returns to nature.

All trace removed of our presence

except our memories,

for whoever else finds this spot of glory.

Frozen socks, scarves, underwear

left overnight on cedar branches

crackle and bend

as they are folded, stiff into ice rimmed packs.


Then we leave

red canoe

yellow canoe

They carry us away to quit

this spit of land next to calling-goose marsh,

and I take from it

a small piece of quartz willingly given.


**The River Almost Claims One**

Log boom travesty

pulls me into the river's embrace.

My feet slip and slide finding no grip

on the ancient cedar chained

to other giants of Mother Earth.

I step out of yellow canoe to balance

on the ancient cedar,

my feet slip, cedar giant twisting and sinking.

I plummet into the river

and call their names to release the icy grip

—Algonquin, Cree, Huron, Ojibway

The cold clutch of the Ottawa River

forces my lungs to gasp,

submerged beneath its amusement

as I kick upwards for air.

I pull the canoe across the ancient cedar.

Frozen dance by the shore

to find dry clothes.

Hands, legs and body

turn purple and blue

this icy morning.

Log boom travesty left behind

we leave calling-goose marsh

in our wake and minds.

We begin to run against rapids

where ospreys have their nest.

Wheeling in the sky

they are of it, gazing down at our struggle

to mount minor rapids.

"Going the wrong way!" the ospreys scream.

They are masters of their domain

only we are not of ours.


Long haul, patient haul,

slowly tiring into Portage-du-Ford,

a central gathering place, once in time,

for coureurs des bois and First Nations.

But now asleep,

No one to notice

No one aware

of our passage

on this First Nations river.


## Listening

Deep into the wilderness,

taking tender care of her,

we clear other people's debris

from our evening resting place.

The forest and river thank us,

for our respect.

## *Past, Present, Future* / Dr. Ian Prattis

Listen—

listen to the sound of it.

listen to the feel of it

raining gently down.

Separating each droplet of rain,

as it enters the womb of earth

through the river.


I partake in its passion.

sitting in the open rain,

my back resting on the yellow canoe

—she supports me always—

wrapped in oilskins to stay dry

drawing the experience of this rain

into every sense of being.


Then we are gone

one yellow canoe

one red

replacing the camp

with our absence.


Presence remains

in individual gratitude

for the intergenerational threads

we are thankful for.

I take from this place,

a white blossom overhanging

the river bank,

and adorn the yellow canoe

with nature's bounty.


## Desolation Song

Deserted river without traffic,

without First Nations, lovers of nature.

Without traders— purveyors of commerce—

this natural highway deserted by humans.

Too early for the snarl and debris

of trippers and cottage dwellers.

The railroad long ago replaced voyageurs.

The loggers and steamships that made fortunes

also gone.


In their absence, we enjoy silence

with this mighty river.

Movement is deserted

save for one yellow canoe, one red.

Four people recreating for themselves

the centuries of Earth beliefs

and hidden threads

through the routes of the past.

The paddle sings high pitched with its tautness,
low toning in the slow arc
of arm and shoulder reach.
The river's song separates the sound of water
rippling from the paddle's entry.
Separate again from the sound
of raindrops dancing and leaping.
Separate songs of one symphony.

Before the rains came today
the sun burnt deep into our bones.
This upper reach of the river
of which I am now a part.
To talk of it, to write of it,
is to dream of it
calling out the past— now in tune.
I catch reflections of yellow canoe
gliding through still water.

## Blinding Torrents

The rain came in torrents
after we traced an osprey's path,
disturbing his fishing.

## *Past, Present, Future* / Dr. Ian Prattis

The osprey strikes

yet misses the trout

sure to be in his talons.

He squawks a high piercing

minor third at us,

imperfect fisher on this day.

He flew from perch to perch,

leading us before taking his leave.


Torrential tsunami.

Too strange a word

for canoes filled with rainwater.

Paddling and bailing the yellow canoe

the raindrops leap into the river

anxious to dance their presence.

We paddled through blinding rain

and unremitting sheets of water,

Abating to a mere downpour,

decreasing to heavy showers

finally diminishing to the respite

of constant drizzle.


The canoes gentled in to a deserted cabin

disturbing an old beaver,

fat from his evening meal of fresh aspen.

He waddled off into the bush

grumbling at our entry.

We needed respite and relief

more than he his aspen.

Paddling through mist bordering swamp,

monotonous muskeg and unrelieved greyness.

Paddles bite into the river.

Canoes lurch without elegance,

losing that free floating glide

that comes with joy.


This gift rediscovered

when our character, deeply hidden,

keeps a plodding, slow progress.

Wet and cold— so cold

until Fort Coulonge, Quebec side

of this river.

Set back, hidden by discrete channels

into which our canoes nosed.

Tying up at the commercial dock

in search of a laundromat

and a place to eat voluminous mounds of food.

To refuel and find our humor.


We sloshed our rain-sodden way

to the spin dryers

divesting ourselves of track shoes,

socks, shirts and all but trousers—into the dryer

amid the sodden reminders

of nature's amusement.

We left—well fed and dry

and found a different response to greyness.


The sun at last came through.

a thick heavy haze, blinding contrast

to the day's grey murky light.

Now our paddles sang.

The canoes glide with new life

surging with joy

finding a following wind

we reached the far side

of Ile Grande Calumette.

Striking camp on the Ontario shore,

frogs chortled in the swamp behind

as we faced the river, below rapids,

too tired to walk

into the woods even a little way.

I prepared a simple table in thy sight,
Ancient Wisdom.

The evening magic passed to nightfall

ere we slept.

## Mohawk Bear

An indigenous friend—Mohawk—

 with the name of a familiar.

Bear

came to our solitude

by this mist laden river

He found us quietly connecting to the past,

with magnificence around and within us.

Bear politely took us from this place

to a bridge close by,

His flatboard truck waiting

to take us to Fort William,

locale of the Hudson Bay Company's past splendor.

A trading post from another era,

once a drawing point for trappers,

hunters, voyageurs, first nations, traders

and river lovers.

All came here in the past for weddings,

furs, funerals and ceremonial feasts.

We stayed this night at the fur trading post.

surrounded by a stand of

red and white pine

tall and majestic.

Nurtured not logged.

I re-peopled with all that was past

—feeling the future's strands unfold as they must.


## The Forest

Whisper of wind through pine needles.

Shimmering aspens and soft poplars of the forest.

Green—spring fresh green,

a relief to the year round darkness of the spruce's

darker timbre and twin pronged sheaths.

The river denies our passage

so we walk through sheltered forests

rather than meet

our death by foolishness.

We find herbs, trilliums white in dense bush,

hiding among the wild strawberries

unbodied with their

rich red summer promise.

Guardian trees, lichen laced,

protest the spring violets pushing upwards.

In the forest a great many entities

of the earth and sky speak of before

and what is to be.

Clearings sunk into the earth

await further visits.

In the center of one clearing

stood a single tall aspen

lonely.

Waiting for companionship,

fragile in its aloneness,

in her aloneness,

in my aloneness.

I stand within her circle

this tree and I

and for a brief moment

neither were alone.

# FUTURE

# 14. Astrophysics and Parallel Universes

Manny Fredericks was of Hopi descent, a brilliant astrophysicist with a distinctive mystical flair. He had published a provocative treatise on parallel universes, which combined astrophysics with traditional indigenous ways of placing energy and intent from one universe to another.

Manny alleged that it was a mystical component that mirrored the Transfer Molecule - a crossover particle that science had long sought in its understanding of co-existing universes. The elusive particle was believed to have properties that enabled it to cross from one universe to another and that such penetration could alter energy patterns.

Astronomer Dr. Tom Hagen was intrigued when he read Fredericks manuscript. A decade before he had, with great urgency, advised the International Space Agency to locate a suitable planet, as habitation on Earth had become increasingly compromised.

Research stations were already orbiting Mars and Jupiter's moon, Europa. Station One at Europa was the key construction. Probes from there were launched into the heliosphere through a wormhole into interstellar space. In a neighboring galaxy, a planet with two moons and a liquid hydrosphere similar to Earth's was located. It was part of an ecliptic plane with a dozen planets orbiting around a massive sequence star, the sun for this system.

The planet located had a liquid hydrosphere similar to Earth. The probes sent back information identifying distinct zones from tropics to poles with evidence of oceans, forests and mountains.

No sign of habitation was revealed, but the probes identified a dense particle field in the upper stratosphere of the planet, similar to a Van Allen belt. The long-term plan was for Europa station to serve as a way station to ferry pioneers to the new planet.

Dr. Hagen immediately tracked Manny through his advanced optic phone. He explained the space project beyond Europa and was surprised to learn that Manny was aware of it. Their conversation focused on the mystical component alluded to in Manny's treatise. They were both excited in their sharing of thoughts. The conversation ended with an invitation for Dr. Hagen to travel to the Hopi Mesas in Northern Arizona. Dr. Hagen jumped at the opportunity, and days later he arrived at Phoenix International Airport.

Manny was waiting for him. He was tall for a Hopi, almost six feet. He wore a white T-shirt with "DON'T WORRY BE HOPI" emblazoned in black across the front. His long black hair was pulled into a pony tail, and his chiseled face lit up with a smile when he saw Dr. Hagen walking towards him, extending his hand in greeting. There was a helicopter from the Space Agency to fly them directly to the Hopi pueblos. On the flight, Manny explained that his people had largely evacuated their villages because the encroaching desert was eroding pastures for their herds of sheep and cattle. Yet one pueblo was still inhabited by elders who kept the ceremonial cycle alive, and indeed developed it further to anticipate the Earth's collapse. There was a cadre of supporters taking care of them. His grandmother had called in the elderly Keepers of the Energies who were patiently waiting for Dr. Hagen and Manny's arrival.

On the flight to Northern Arizona, Manny provided a brief overview of Hopi cosmology. Dr. Hagen was intrigued as he listened intently, fascinated at the year-round ceremonial cycle that challenged humans to develop through intricate and complex rituals. Generations of anthropologists who had researched the Hopi were baffled by this intricacy, not realizing that the obstacle to understanding was their lack of mystical grounding. Manny presented a rhythm of life through the chasm of disbelief, feeling certain that he and Dr. Hagen would be instrumental in closing the lack of knowledge. He confided that he and Dr. Hagen had already been "seen" by the elders, who were waiting for the cosmic order to unfold.

Manny asked Dr. Hagen through the headphones, "Do you have the co-ordinates for the new planet's location? My grandmother will need to know that very precisely." Dr. Hagen did have the location specs but wondered why an elderly Hopi elder would need them. He did not voice his query, but Manny picked up on the concern.

"Dr. Hagen, do not be fooled by my grandmother when you meet her. She has a master's degree in both mathematics and quantum physics. She has already made it clear what she needs from you. She may look like a traditional elder, but there is much more to her than that."

Manny provided further information about this formidable woman.

"When she graduated from MIT her professors begged her to continue to a Ph.D., as they had rarely encountered a mind like hers. She declined, as her life trajectory was ceremonial, creating new vistas for harmony with what she knew from science and her tradition. Her entire thesis was grounded in ceremonial principles and built with impeccable logic to move the boundaries of understanding. She provided a new level of expression and intent and was the impetus for me to write the article that brought you here. You will find her an extraordinary woman."

Dr. Hagen nodded and changed the focus by asking Manny whether he was choosing science over ceremonial. Manny gave Dr. Hagen a broad grin.

"With a grandmother like mine, there was no choice to make. While I am devoted to science and love it, I do know where my starting point is. And if I ever forget, I have that steel trap mind of my grandmother to deal with."

Manny dug into his pocket and pulled out an envelope addressed to Dr. Hagen. "My grandmother has a message for you. Here it is."

Dr. Hagen carefully opened the envelope and stared at the neat handwriting.

*My grandson is integral to the ceremony we will create. It is necessary for him to accompany you on the journey to the new planet. He has the knowledge to provide a foundation for your enterprise. You will need him.*

This note was not a request. Dr. Hagen also intuited that he was about to face the largest leap of faith in his entire life. He carefully tucked the note inside his jacket pocket and asked Manny to provide some details of the ceremony that was being prepared by the Hopi elders. Manny composed himself and placed his mind in his grandmother's and began to speak the words she would use.

"There are four Sacred Keepers, and that includes her. They have already prepared the kiva for a new departure in their ceremonial cycle. The kiva is a large underground ceremonial chamber, like a womb in the Earth body. It enables life and death to enfold in seamless continuity. It is built of stone and placed in the central plaza of the pueblo in accordance with the four directions: North, East, South and West. The ceremony will take place in the underground chamber. It has a sunken fire pit in the center which will be used as the central circle of a medicine wheel constructed in the kiva for the first time. My grandmother felt this was essential. Access to the kiva is by means of a ladder reaching into the upper chamber, which pokes up four to five feet above ground. This architecture is the heart of Hopi cosmology."

He placed his hand on the medicine pouch at his belt that he had received from his grandmother when he was a young initiate into the mysteries. Manny paused for several minutes, as though he was listening to her voice before continuing the education of Dr. Hagen.

"In the ceremonial chamber, my grandmother has created a sand painting using traditional symbols for animals, sea and lake creatures, corn seeds and plants, sky and earth. She has added new symbols for your spaceship and the new planet. You may understand now why she needs to know the precise location. You must inform her when you meet."

Dr. Hagen leaned closer to Manny as he listened. Manny explained that the four Sacred Keepers were unanimous in their enthusiasm for the interstellar venture. Manny's grandmother was the Keeper of the Sky People and would be sitting at the North stone of the medicine wheel. She would track and find the energy passage to the new planet once she was provided with its location specs. The Keeper of the Animals was already gathering his essential energy to transport it through time and space. He would be at the East stone. The Keeper of Corn, Plants and Trees had spoken with these particular families and requested their co-operation, which was granted. That Sacred Keeper, a seasoned woman elder, would sit at the South stone.

The Keeper of the Earth would be located at the West stone for her to usher in the energy of new beginnings."

Manny's eyes glistened with tears as he realized the immensity of what the Hopi elders were offering.

"I will be at the fire pit in the center of the chamber. My task is to keep the inside circle of the medicine wheel open so there is a portal for the energies to pour through to their new destination on the planet. The Sacred Keeper at the East stone will also concentrate on the spirit world energies to assist me. My grandmother called me in to do this, as I have been trained by her and have the spiritual strength to hold the portal open. The four Sacred Keepers have specific energies to concentrate upon and send them through the portal."

The tears had not stopped as Manny said,

"The Keepers are elderly, all in their 80's, and I now realize that this ceremony is their last before departing this life."

They were both silent with the realization that the Four Sacred Keepers were offering their lives to enable a renewal on a distant planet that none of them would experience.

Dr. Hagen asked, "Manny, will you survive the ceremony?"

The sound of the helicopter's blades was all that could be heard as Manny remained silent. Eventually he answered, "No, I will not die in the sacred kiva. I am coming with you to the new planet. You did get the instruction from my grandmother did you not?"

They both allowed a grim smile but were overwhelmed by the intentions of the four elderly Sacred Keepers of the Hopi. The helicopter hovered over the dusty main plaza in

Orobai, the only inhabited pueblo. The Hopi villages clung precariously to six-hundred-foot-high escarpments looming out of the desert terrain, distributed on three rocky mesas. The buildings in Orobai pueblo seemed surreal as they poked out of the desert surrounding the escarpment. Sunlight glinted on old pickup trucks and barely into the remaining dwellings which were shuttered against the desert. Several horses could be seen tethered in a dusty compound.

They could see a gathering of people off to one side of the plaza where the helicopter put down to the north of the kiva. Orobai pueblo was the root of the annual cycle of ceremonies and this was where the remaining elders and their supporters now lived. The four Sacred Keepers were wearing traditional garments—white tunics with dazzling Hopi woven blankets thrown over the shoulder. Their demeanor, a calm and unworldly steadiness, struck Dr. Hagen forcibly as he looked at the four incredible people who had offered to help his mission. He was introduced to Manny's grandmother and the three other Sacred Keepers. They had dark, wrinkled faces and they spoke to Manny in the deep, guttural manner of ancient times. He sensed their all-seeing wisdom and deep stillness. They had something about them that was outside of time and space and it cast an eerie presence that made Dr. Hagen shiver in the heat of the desert.

When he looked into the eyes of Manny's grandmother, Dr. Hagen sank to his knees before her. She calmly held out her hands to him and stood before him. He looked into the eyes of wisdom, beauty and power. She spoke to him in perfect English.

"I hope that Manny has instructed you well." She chuckled with that deep guttural sound he had heard before. "You have the new planet's location for me?"

Dr. Hagen nodded. There was nothing he could say.

She understood and said, "We know what is to be created here and treat it as an honor to be part of it. I will introduce you to the other Keepers."

Dr. Hagen was included in a circle of the most magnificent people he had ever met. The tears continued to flow down his face.

"This is good," remarked Manny's grandmother. "Do not lament that we will not return from the kiva," she said. "I reassure you that this is what we want. We are ready to move on and become part of the Sky People. That is something all four of us have yearned for. We gladly reach for that transformation. We cannot invite you into the kiva. You must stay outside, next to where the North stone is placed. I will show you."

She took Dr. Hagen by the hand and pointed to the chair placed above the North stone in the subterranean chamber.

She seemed quite precise and said, "We will be inside with the ceremony for the rest of the day. It will be completed by morning. You are to stay at this location throughout. Our people will bring you water and sustenance. At daybreak, Manny will come out by the ladder. There is a flat stone that fits the top of the kiva perfectly. You and Manny will place that over the entrance, as this kiva becomes our tomb, though only for our dead bodies. We will have gone elsewhere by dawn."

She looked deeply into Dr. Hagen's eyes, and he felt he was looking into universe after universe.

"I have one request. Do not ask Manny what took place in the ceremonial chamber of the kiva. When the time is right, he will inform you. Until that time, please resist all curiosity about the Transfer Particle. The fact that you land safely on the new planet in the next galaxy is proof enough."

Dr. Hagen relaxed for the first time,

"I now understand Manny's reference to your steel trap logic!"

She smiled again, and he felt the deep love she extended to him and to all beings. She summoned her three companions, and they nimbly climbed down the ladder into the womb of the Earth. Manny was the last to enter the kiva, pulling a wood and vine cover over the opening. Dr. Hagen took up his station at the North apex, and, for the first time in a long while, he began to pray.

He was not particularly spiritual, but at that moment he became so. He remembered the chants and sutras from his flirtation with Buddhism much earlier in life, reflecting on the teachings of impermanence and emptiness. In that long night under the desert stars, he internalized what he had ignored for so long. He knew that his contribution to the Four Sacred Keepers was stillness and the absence of thought.

He allowed his scientific mind to recede and felt deeply in his body the unification of universes. Dr. Hagen opened up to the reality of something of which he had no prior knowledge. The taste of the burning fire pit at the center of the medicine wheel was pungent in his mouth.

Although the night was cold, beads of sweat broke out on his forehead and ran down his cheeks, splashing onto his buttoned shirt. He was starkly aware that the Sacred Keeper of the Sky People was directly below him.

Manny's grandmother had given him specific instructions, and he kept to them as though they were sacred vows.

He was in unfamiliar territory, which became more and more unusual as the night proceeded. Yet he was prepared to make that leap of faith to trust completely the elderly Hopi elders who were offering their lives.

Deep sobs arose in his chest and he cried uncontrollably several times during that long dark night.

The first light of dawn on the desert horizon was not a relief, just a marker of the most significant act of his life. The morning breeze raised a brief sand storm.

He gripped the wood of the sturdy chair upon which he sat. He felt the knots of the hard wood with his two hands. This grounded him deeply in the experience of the four Sacred Keepers who he knew were now dead. Humbled by their nobility, he waited patiently.

He made it through the rest of the night until he heard Manny's steps on the ladder and was there to embrace him as he climbed out of the sacred kiva. His new friend looked gaunt and bereft yet had a steely determination in his eyes.

Between them they lifted the stone slab and placed it on the opening of the kiva. They sat at the North apex where Dr. Hagen had been stationed, very quiet, full of wonder and grief.

Breakfast was brought over to them by the remaining elders of the pueblo, who knew what had taken place. The coffee was good, as were the corn tortillas. There was no need for any conversation or analysis.

Dr. Hagen and Manny climbed into the helicopter and were quickly ferried to Phoenix International Airport. It was a silent journey.

Both men knew they had been radically changed and readied for the voyage to the new planet.

# 15. The Last Man on the Planet

British actor, Pete Postlethwaite, plays the best role of his acting career in the film, *"The Age of Stupid."* The only fictional character in this riveting film, he plays the part of an old man living alone in the High Arctic in a world totally decimated by global warming and pandemic.

In the movie, humanity had allowed the environment to become an extension of egocentric needs and values—an ego-sphere rather than an eco-sphere. In this ego-sphere, people consumed mindlessly throughout the globe without any regard for ecosystem balance.

There was no concern for inequality, poverty and starvation. Planetary and personal care was not on this agenda, as the film graphically shows.

The old man, the last person on the planet, is the curator of The Global Archive digital storage laboratory. He sits in his home and watches archival videos.

The footage he views shows global warming reaching tipping points and runaway effects. He wonders how the human mind could be capable of monumental achievements while neglecting to prevent the destruction of their ecosystem. The old man shakes his head in disbelief. The movie poses a stark question: Why didn't we stop climate change when there was a chance to make the leap to a zero-net-carbon world?

The director of the film, Fanny Armstrong, creates a montage from live news and documentaries. She illuminates the steps into global decline and the devastation for human habitation and other species.

In an artfully created mosaic, six real-life characters play out the dramas of their personal stories. Their humanity and stupidity are extant in this brilliant tapestry of human folly. Ultimately, the film gives us an answer - OIL! Our dependence on it, addiction to it, and our refusal to move away from a carbon-fueled lifestyle propelled the downward spiral of devastation.

What is so gripping is that we who view the real life characters are made to feel distinctly uncomfortable. Their shadows and myopia reflect our own shadows and myopia, especially those of our political and corporate leaders. After watching this film we can no longer hide. We are held to account as this film becomes our story. It is impossible not to be moved – hopefully to a constructive direction of immediate action.

"*The Age of Stupid*" is a watershed film for our species. Rather than moving away from a carbon-fueled lifestyle, humanity chose the opposite trajectory, which brought a rapid increase in climate change and greenhouse gases. Big Oil and government propaganda promoted oil and gas extraction, irrespective of the damage to ecosystems and populations. In particular they produced false images of reforestation - utmost safety *they said*, deep concern for wildlife *they said*, populations and clean water *they said*.

Decades later we find those rivers and lakes becoming wastelands. Oil derivatives swiftly poured through interconnected waterways and indigenous populations who once augmented their households with fish, game and forest products, relocated or died. Degradation of the Earth's ecology was the catalyst for radical climate catastrophe compounded by severe pandemics.

Scientists, way back in 1979 and 1980, attempted to divert the catastrophe with a clear grasp of what *was* causing climate crisis. A small group of scientists, politicians and activists in America came to a broad understanding of the causes and dynamics of climate change. Scientists had realized that the more carbon dioxide pouring into the atmosphere, the warmer Earth would become. And, in doing so, it would trigger a violent atmospheric wrecking of the planet. They placed their findings and consensus to the highest levels of government and industry in the United States and around the world.

The scientists included James Hansen, NASA climate studies; Gordon MacDonald, geophysicist; Jule Charney, meteorologist; Steve Schneider, environmental biologist; George Woodall, ecologist and many more world class scientists.

Politicians such as Al Gore and lobbyist Rafe Pomerance took the scientific findings to the White House and to energy giants such as Exxon. The latter were distinctly uncomfortable about how much they would be blamed for climate change.

Despite their early support, the energy giants quickly turned to finding mouthpieces who would state that the scientific findings were not translatable into global disasters.

The scientists were lobbying based on meticulous scientific findings. Their emphasis to politicians and industry was about the freezing of carbon emissions and the development of alternative energies that did not create carbon dioxide. At that time, some forty years ago, it seemed to be a good idea to many world leaders. A consensus-based plan, however, would not happen without American leadership. The United States was the obvious nation to lead such an outcome. It failed to do so, much to the chagrin and reputation of the scientists, as their findings were censored and belittled. They then became targets that the carbon cabal sought to undermine.

Two Forks in the Road—Which Will We Take?

If we continue to turn our beautiful rivers into sewers because of our endless greed and neglectful ignorance, there is no place on Mother Earth to sustain our present civilization. If human consciousness is too slow to make a quantum leap to a culture of sustainability, then there are drastic consequences to contemplate. All of which are starkly portrayed in the film, *"The Age of Stupid."*

"Failsafe" is an engineering term used to describe a lever or stop valve that comes into action when a piece of machinery is about to self-destruct. The lever comes down or the stop valve kicks in before the nuclear core melts down into inevitable destruction. I talked about the Failsafe in Consciousness concept in my book *Failsafe: Saving the Earth from Ourselves*. It describes how human consciousness will be held back by a deliberately cultivated ignorance about better knowledge. And so, the global ecological situation deteriorates to a breaking point. My thought was that such breaking points, however, could also act as a catalyst, exposing greed and ignorance. At which point consciousness could be propelled into expansion, deliberation and change.

My vision was a positive one, as I believed that humanity could create solutions to address ecological emergency. We have the knowledge to create this, but the obstacles that stand in the way are not technological or scientific. They are the attitudes, values and concepts that define the present dominance of corporate values. I argued that the necessary clarity to deal with global environmental crises will emerge, once our thoughts, values and attitudes no longer sustain our internal pollution. This is the radical, internal climate change necessary to engage intelligently with the external climate change.

There is certainly global awareness, but also fear about the future of planet Earth. The overwhelming terror of Gaia crashing down on us is unbearable.

Many years ago in India I had an audience with Sai Baba. I was visiting this sage's ashram in Andra Pradesh with an Indian friend. As Sai Baba walked slowly through the morning gathering, to my utter surprise he stopped in front of me. He spoke to me for quite a while. Somehow he knew of my commitment to environmental concerns. I remember very little of what was said, except for one sentence that blazed into my mind and stayed there. Sai Baba said to me that a transformation in human consciousness required 2% of the world's population to meditate on a daily basis. I have no clue about the knowledge source for his pronouncement, but I vividly remember the "buzz" of energy in my mind and body.

I translated Sai Baba's wisdom into a 2% option. If only I, and others, could encourage 2% of the people we knew to change their lifestyles to one of voluntary simplicity – then we could mitigate the environmental crisis. The planet would then remain habitable for all species. This would involve conserving energy usage, being aware of the effects of mindless consumerism, and completing one eco-friendly action every day.

This may seem naïve, but to me the 2% option was easily within everyone's grasp. The end result of such a transformed consciousness would lead to different questions being asked, creating different solutions and structures.

There would be a new mindset to make the necessary decisions for change. This statement from Sai Baba changed my thoughts about awakening.

Not everyone has to "wake up" - just 2%. This spearhead could provide the strategic tipping point for a positive change in planetary care.

This brings me back to *"The Age of Stupid"* as a watershed film. You will not be the same after you have seen it. I refer the reader to *Failsafe's* Appendix I: Simple Steps to Empowerment, which provides an action plan for the global ecological emergency. The steps are:

Take Action

Get Up Close And Personal

Reduce Your Ecological Footprint

Guidelines for Business and the Workplace

The "Big" Picture for The Future

Science and Diversity

Environmental Organizations

Warning to Governments

If only we can get it right and get it right now! The best-case scenario is that we get on with the task of reining in our egos and greed-driven minds. This then permits a Failsafe in Consciousness to kick in, because the conditions and opening have been created by our choice to cultivate different patterns within our minds.

Consciousness expansion can no longer be held back as the radical *internal* climate change takes over. Our innate knowledge is manifest, and we interconnect with a vast counterculture that is no longer a minority.

We become another light shining in the quiet revolution that has over two million organizations worldwide pursuing constructive change.

This hopeful trajectory is that our diligent, mindful engagement will change our brain structures to permit the formation of new paradigms of behavior. As cells in the ecosystem of Gaia, it is as though humanity has aligned their neuronal networks with principles of ecosystem balance, ethics and responsibility.

The critical mass has arrived, and it amounts to a collective tipping point for our species. Once the negative mind is reined in, then clarity and compassion provide the basis for how we can exist with the planet and with one another in a totally new way. This happens if we "Begin It Now"—the concluding words to *Failsafe: Saving the Earth From Ourselves.*

The Second Fork: A Failed Genetic Experiment

I underestimated, however, the lure and power of the second fork. We are, in fact, our environment. It is our collective habits, thoughts and patterns that have created a flimsy, uncertain future for our species.

Every authoritative body on the planet provides dire warnings to humanity about the effects of climate change. It is clear that our current non-sustainable energy and economic systems are not working. It is also clear that pathological consumerism is a major behavioral manifestation of industrial civilization.

Because of all the warning signals, allow me to be starkly realistic. If the Failsafe in Consciousness does not kick in, the field is open for billions of us to die in an intolerable climate. Perhaps, after all, the Arctic Circle may not be such a bad evolutionary staging point. Digital records, carefully preserved as archaeological relics, could provide clear guidelines for future civilizations to conduct themselves more appropriately with respect to the Earth Mother.

I finish with Dave Hampton's passionate thoughts about this film (Resurgence May/June 2009: 66).

*"The Age of Stupid* is not just a film that could change the course of humanity. I hope it will be the catalyst that gives us a second chance to create a sustainable future. I hope it will promote a mass collective awakening globally such that we are not stupid and that we choose life and reclaim our children's birthright - the right to expect a future."

I have fourteen grandchildren.

In the same vein as this film, I wrote this essay "The Last Man on the Planet." Consider it as archival footage from present time that provides an action plan so that my grandchildren may enjoy a habitable planet. Should the adversity of climate change overwhelm humanity then a different question arises.

*What will we choose as a paradigm of behavior?*


Glance at the sun

*See the moon*

*And the stars*

*Gaze at the beauty*

*Of the Earth's*

*Greening*

*Now Think*


*Hildergard of Bingen 1098–1179*

# 16. Jihadist Hijack

Several years after the space settlements were established on Planet Horizon, Captain Marshall, Special Forces, received this encrypted message from Planet Earth:

International Space Agency, China - ALERT

Jihadists hijacked spaceship HORIZON ONE at Planet Earth launch facility in China. Pilot and navigator are sleeper members of a jihadist cell. Massacre at launch facility and destruction of communication systems. Fourteen jihadists, eight men and six women, heavily armed, well trained and dangerous. Intent to take over Planet Horizon. Space Agency is readying spacecraft HORIZON TWO with weaponry.

Spacecraft HORIZON ONE had 50 pioneers for Horizon Planet. All massacred at Earth Station. Do not underestimate jihadist intentions to take over. They have sleepers in your community. HORIZON ONE spacecraft has wormhole and Horizon Planet co-ordinates logged into navigation system. Jihadist pilot and navigator know how to get through interstellar space and where to land on your planet. Ten days before they arrive.

IMPERATIVE - CHECK PIONEER COMMUNITY FOR SLEEPERS.

Captain Marshall decoded the encrypted message and immediately sent an urgent message to Dr. Hansen, chef-de-mission, and to his Special Forces unit. Dr. Edith Thompson, the mission empath and clairvoyant, joined the tense gathering to listen to the communique.

Dr. Hansen was a tall commanding figure, his thinning hair offset by deep flinty eyes that he now fixed on Edith. Hansen looked at her, once Marshall finished speaking.

"Edith, with your extrasensory capabilities could you go over each pioneer on Horizon who could be a sleeper? We must find the enemy within first of all."

She calmly assented and glanced up at the sun beams dancing on the table in front of her. She was responsible for creating eco-towns on Horizon for a thousand people. Edith noticed the sultry day, cooling down in the evening under a subtropical sun.

She carried her Celtic heritage gently and obviously. The traits of mysticism were very strong in her. She was slender with auburn hair streaked with grey. Her hazel eyes could be soft and gentle, then hawk-like in an instant.

Her diplomacy and grace convened the community councils where everyone had a voice to frame intentions, priorities and policies. Edith took a deep breath and closed her eyes. She scanned every wave of pioneers searching for anything that felt out of place.

Everyone stayed very quiet, until her eyes opened wide, "There is a couple from Venezuela, who do not feel like a couple at all, always on the edge of community. Like a masquerade."

She looked intensely at Marshall and Hansen, "They are not alone, but we must be skillful how we can find that out. The man's name is Miguel, a skilled engineer and irrigation specialist. His wife is Rebecca, a nurse."

Marshall and Hansen immediately left and checked first that Miguel and Rebecca were not at home. They searched their cabin, meticulously going over its simple contents.

They found a grey metal case underneath their bed. Hansen forced the locked case open to reveal a cache of sophisticated light weight weapons - grenade launchers, laser weapons and hand guns. They wondered how the weapons had been smuggled on previous spaceships.

Marshall carefully removed the weapons. They replaced the metal case under the bed and waited inside for the couple's return. Miguel and Rebecca entered the cabin just before supper time to find their own weapons pointed at their heads. Their hands and legs were then tightly bound.

Hansen conducted the questions, which he asked in English.

"Why do you have grenade launchers and weapons in your quarters? Do you really come from Venezuela, or are you from somewhere else?"

Miguel stared at him with contempt before stating, "You do not know who you are dealing with. We were born into jihadism, just as our ancestors were born into jihadism. Like them we entered *Shahadah* with vengeance in our hearts. This declaration of faith is to avenge the injustice of your people against ours. Our uprising will continue for as many centuries as it takes to eliminate your evil culture. Whether on Earth or here on this new planet, Jihadism will prevail and conquer. *La ilaha illa Allah* There is no God but Allah."

Hansen calmly pointed out that the people on Horizon were international and had not participated in any injustice towards their people. Miguel carelessly spoke rapidly to Rebecca in Arabic, not realizing that Hansen was fluent in three Middle East languages. They inadvertently revealed two other sleepers. Hansen remained calm and continued to ask questions in English.

"Are there other members of your jihadist cell in the Oasis community? What were you intending to do with these weapons?"

Miguel had already spoken to Rebecca about a rendezvous with a jihadist Dutch couple, Joel and his wife Agnes. Miguel again spoke in Arabic to Rebecca, indicating that Joel would know something was wrong, as he was to meet him after supper to receive instructions. Hansen then asked if they had suffered any discrimination while in Oasis village. Miguel glared at him and spat in his direction. Hansen carefully wiped the spittle from his face with a piece of cloth.

He smiled at both captives and spoke in fluent Arabic, "*Asalaamu Alikum* Peace Be Upon You. Thank you for leading us to your partners. You will stay here under house arrest, while we pay a visit to Joel and Agnes. They too will be placed under house arrest, *Inshallah* God Willing."

Miguel was furious. He tried to stand and head butt Hansen but a swift elbow from Marshall to his temple felled him on the spot. Hansen intimated to Rebecca not to follow her partner's intent and alerted Marshall about where Joel and Agnes had their home. Their cabin was empty and while Marshall searched for, and found, a similar cache of weapons, Special Forces apprehended Joel and Agnes in the dining room and brought them back to their cabin. They had their hands bound behind their backs and their ankles lashed together.

The interrogation was by Marshall. He was courteous and soft spoken. As a trained sniper, he placed himself in calm states that kept his green eyes opened wide, missing nothing. Meticulous and shrewd, he was several steps ahead of his prisoners.

"We know your jihadist cell has hijacked the HORIZON ONE spacecraft that is due here in ten days. They massacred all personnel at the Earth Station in China." He stopped to ensure that he was in command of his emotions. He looked at both of them, surprised that these Dutch agronomists, who had worked so hard to establish irrigation systems for Oasis village, intended to harm them.

"Was it your intention to kill fellow pioneers when the spaceship landed here?"

"We do not have fellow pioneers," sneered Joel. "You are unbelievers and will die when we take over. Those that wish to convert to *Sharia* Law will live a different life than they do now."

Marshall calmly inquired, "Why do you think anyone will convert to your twisted vision of Islam? You persist with an outdated ideology that is not welcome to most Muslims, let alone the pioneers here."

Joel's face flushed, and he began a tirade about western unbelievers and the ultimate supremacy of jihadism. Marshall interrupted the flow of obscenity by pointing out the considerable non-western component of pioneers around them.

Hansen had sat observing the Dutch couple while Marshall questioned. After listening to their well-rehearsed script, he quietly entered the conversation.

"*Allahu Akbar* God is Great. We are on the new planet of Horizon in the late part of the twenty first century. You present a distorted version of Islam that has no foundation in the teachings of the Prophet Mohammed." His quiet voice immediately got their attention.

"You reflect a dichotomy of *Darul Islam,* living inside Muslim countries as opposed to *Darul Harb,* which refers to territories of war dominated by non-Muslims. This artifice is not found in the formative principles of Islam. The basis of your call to arms by jihadist leaders is stuck in a past that does not exist, and certainly does not belong in the future."

"How dare you insult our beliefs," Agnes exploded.

Hansen quietly observed the young woman and wondered where her sweet demeanor had gone. He remembered her, seemingly happy, when he worked alongside her building the irrigation system at the Oasis village. But something deeper and dangerous about her was carefully hidden. In a measured tone and logic, Hansen pointed out that she and her partner were ignorant about the beliefs that had led them to a readiness to kill neighbors.

He continued, "In the present era *Darul Islam* and *Darul Harb* are spiritually bankrupt, replaced in modern Islam by the term *Darul Aman* where secular laws in other countries are seen as similar to core principles of Islam. This reality has been totally distorted by your jihadist perspective."

Joel and Agnes were shocked by Dr. Hagen's words, as he continued speaking.

"The emergence of *Darul Aman* provided direction for Muslims to coexist with non-Muslims. It is a charter supported throughout the Qur'an where Muslims are free to practice their faith, and, at the same time, obey the laws of the land. He quoted instances of this from the Qur'an (2.177) "It is not righteousness to turn your face towards East or West, but rather righteousness is … to fulfill the contracts which you make."

Joel screamed in rage at him, "Do not quote my faith to me, you bastard."

Hansen responded, "It would seem that you know less than I about the contents of the Qur'an." He allowed a minute to pass before continuing.

"You are ignorant, out of date and not intelligent about the Prophet's teachings. It is hard for me to understand such persistence with a flawed ideology."

His serene composure enraged Joel, who tried to stand up and lash out at him but succeeded only on falling on the cabin floor. Hansen spoke directly to the fallen prisoner in the same calm manner.

"Instead of creating modern solutions to keep your faith and the laws of the country you are in, jihadism placed you in a mediaeval context that is irrelevant. You are locked into ancient stereotypes that were useless in the Middle Ages and totally obsolete in present time."

He paused for a moment before driving the stake in,

"What mental pathologies did you have before jihad? What teachers did you study with to learn the noble and wise teachings of the Prophet Mohammed? *Allahu Akbar?*"

Any composure that Joel had maintained quickly vanished with these goads. His anger rose as he began to swear and curse, promising death and torture to every pioneer he could get his hands on. He stopped only when his long and vicious outburst exhausted him, as subtropical darkness began to envelop the cabin.

Hansen retained his steely calm, "Nobody here at Oasis has been unkind to you. No one has discriminated against you. You are free to express your faith as you please providing you abide by community rules. This example of conduct is upheld in the Qur'an. Yet you are prepared to open fire and kill us when your jihadist comrades arrive here on HORIZON ONE."

He paused to allow this to sink in to the prisoners.

"Do you not remember the vision expressed by Dr. Edith Thompson at a community council you both were present at? She said, 'We wish to establish a community here that takes care of the environment, bound by caring and sharing for one another just as we care for the ecology of this new planet.' You have been embraced by this ethic ever since you arrived on this new planet."

Agnes shouted at him, "Shut your filthy mouth. How dare a piece of shit like you speak the name of our Prophet? You will be the first one I shoot."

Hansen realized he had successfully rattled their self-assurance and permitted a broad smile in their direction before addressing them once more,

"Thank you both for revealing so much. Your ignorance and pathology are evident. I will return tomorrow to provide further lessons on the teachings of the Prophet Mohammed."

Marshall did his best to prevent a smile from appearing on his face, for he realized that Hansen was not finished speaking to the Dutch couple.

Hansen spoke, "Before I leave you, realize that breaking the contract of being here at Oasis village is *haram,* absolutely forbidden by core Islamic principles. You have transgressed Islamic Law. But rest assured, you will not be executed or harmed, which is what your misguided version of *Shariah* Law would do. The Oasis community will find a solution for you and your two comrades to thrive on territory you can call your own. As a community we will greet your deadly intent with generosity and opportunity. The rest will be up to you. I take my leave. *Asalaamu Akbar.*"

Marshall left the cabin with Hansen as two Special Force soldiers took guard of the prisoners. Marshall exclaimed as soon as they were out of earshot, "That was masterful. Where did you learn so much about Islam?"

Hansen smiled, "My university studies were in astrophysics and religion. I also focused on learning Arabic and other languages from that region." He grimaced as he took in a long breath between his teeth and let out his frustration on the out breath.

"These two were easy to crack as they were not brought up in the jihadist culture of Miguel and Rebecca, who in fact come from the tribal area of Northern Syria. They were sent to Venezuela to obtain credentials to infiltrate this hijack mission. The home-grown jihadists are well organized and highly trained. They could not be broken down so easily as the Dutch pair. But it is clear that we needed much better screening for the first coterie of pioneers to come to this planet."

Both couples were placed under house arrest and the ripples of disbelief, anger and betrayal travelled quickly through the Oasis community. Hansen and Marshall called the community together that same evening. Everyone came. There was heated discussion about deadly retaliation upon the four jihadist sleepers amongst them, but Edith Thompson, the empath, cautioned restraint.

"Dear ones, retaliation is not the route to take. We will defend ourselves against the jihadist attack emanating from the arrival of HORIZON ONE, but the four people under house arrest will not be executed." She paused to allow her heartfelt words to sink in to everyone's mind.

There was a shout from the back…. "They were going to execute as many of us on the ground as they could. They cannot get away with that betrayal and potential violence."

Edith said, "I feel despair at the betrayal just as you do. I understand the deadly fear that four members of our community were willing to murder us when the spacecraft arrives. I resent this deeply, just as everyone here does, but we must distinguish ourselves from their hate."

She took another deep breath as what she was about to say pained her deeply, "The jihadists onboard the spaceship do not know that their comrades, planted in our midst, are under house arrest. We must formulate a strategic plan to defeat them. There is no reasoning with them that will work. I wish there was a way, as that suits my preference, but the wave of massacres following the jihadists on board HORIZON ONE rules out that possibility. That must be clear to everyone. For the four jihadists under arrest in Oasis, I propose that we find a place for them to live on their own, far away from us and without their weapons. We have worked alongside them, and, though they mean us harm, we must be compassionate. They can thrive in their own way if they choose to."

Marshall was in agreement and said, "From the drone data we have examined, there is a large island some hundred kilometers from here. There is water and land that looks fertile with varieties of tropical fruit-bearing trees. We can take them there, still bound and under arrest, and leave them with rations, plants and tools. That is a first consideration for all of us to endorse. What matters next is how to defeat the spaceship jihadists."

Hansen said, "I have seen the devastating power of the laser tools that Marshall has created. We have four laser tools. They can be connected together as one device and placed with explosives on the spaceship landing rock and ignited when HORIZON ONE comes to settle down."

Marshall was quick to respond, "Yes, I can do that from an electronic detonating devise some distance away."

He then brought military order to the proceedings.

"We have sophisticated laser weapons taken from the captives. The grenade launchers are top-of-the-line weapons. Once the hatch of the spacecraft opens, Special Forces will fire each grenade launcher in a sequence of mere seconds between each grenade. We have four grenades and know how to use them. Additional Special Forces with sniper rifles will be the second sphere of attack. Then radiating out from the landing spot, we must dig a circle of deep pits with sharpened stakes pointing upwards. The pits will be concealed by a frame covered in vines and branches. If any jihadist gets beyond the pits, in addition to the snipers we will have thirty archers ready as there are no other weapons. Set further back will be a triage area for anyone who is wounded, as we must expect casualties. The jihadists will be heavily armed and never forget that they are highly trained and deadly in their intent to kill us."

Marshall looked around at the intense faces of his friends.

"Our singular advantage is the element of surprise and the fact that support on the ground is no longer a danger to us. Is this all clear to everyone?" It was.

Marshall outlined his plan: "I will need teams to dig the pits and place strong sharpened stakes in them. Special Forces will be first in line with the grenade launchers at the landing pad, so we will build defensive rock walls in front of us. The archers will begin daily target practice."

There was a deep, silent hush once Marshall stopped barking out his orders. His military mind was fully engaged. Hansen could see the determination in the faces of their friends. No one was going to take away what they had built on Horizon.

He said, "This forthcoming battle marks the end of our innocence. With the loss of innocence comes further wisdom, rather than hate. We have ten days to prepare. Marshall's strategy is sound, and we must perfect the timing. Edith is correct about how to treat the threat from within."

He stopped to allow his words to sink in to the minds of his friends.

"We are defending one another so that once this is over, we can go about building community with eyes wide open rather than half shut. We have work to do and much to organize."

During that time, Hansen felt moments of utter dismay that there was no escape from fractious fanaticism. Their former planet, Earth, had been destroyed by greed and disorder. The frequent news was always of further deterioration and world-wide conflict driven by corporations and fanatics seeking possession over scarce resources. That survival reality had now caught up with them as they knew the hijacked spaceship was approaching their new planet. They prepared well and trained meticulously over the next ten days, waiting for the imminent battle. Then to everyone's surprise the battle was over in a matter of minutes

Hansen waited intensely for the jihadist pilot to reverse the spacecraft engines for HORIZON ONE to slowly come closer to the solid rock. The spaceship hovered ten feet above the ground. The support legs were extended to stabilize the spaceship on the sculpted plane of hard rock that served as a landing pad. Marshall got Hansen's signal to detonate the four lasers, creating a devastating explosion that ripped through the rear of the spacecraft. With the four lasers exploding underneath the engines, the spacecraft toppled slowly to the left of the landing pad.

The space hatch opened, and heavily armed jihadists rushed out shooting their high-powered laser weapons in all directions. Before they could move down the ladder, they were met by accurately fired grenades, launched by the weapons held by Special Forces. They fired four grenades at intervals and decimated the armed force intent on killing them. Each grenade exploded, scattering titanium shrapnel with deadly effect inside the confined space of HORIZON ONE.

Eight armed jihadists managed to break through the grenade barrage and reached the edge of the landing pad only to stumble into deep concealed pits with sharpened poles upon which they impaled themselves. Marshall, spotting the fallen jihadists through binoculars, shouted that there were two left. The pilot and navigator took their time before stepping out of the open hatch with their hands in the air. Through his binoculars he could see they were wearing suicide vests. On his instruction the snipers swiftly took them down. One of the vests exploded and accounted for the sure death of both of them.

 Not a single pioneer was killed, though a stray bullet from a falling jihadist had caught Marshall in the shoulder. His flesh wound was the only casualty. The archers had killed two jihadists who managed to crawl out of the death pits. The eight men and six women jihadists on board HORIZON ONE were all dead.

Marshall insisted on a debriefing, yet it turned into a retrospective examination of why they were on Horizon and whether their communal values were compromised.

There was a clear sky overhead and a fresh breeze coming from the ocean, a rebuke to the violence in which they had participated. The consensus was that their actions this day were to preserve their original vision. There was a fierce feeling that evening from the manner they had prepared for battle and how they stood and fought together.

There was genuine compassion on the next day, as the four sleeper jihadists were led to the community's helicopter. The four had to take a long walk, shuffling between two lines of pioneers who had once thought of them as friends. There was no hate, cursing or shouting at them, just a silent regret.

The four prisoners screamed and yelled expletives in English and Arabic, though they slowly came to a stop when no one reacted to their abusive language. The jihadists painfully shuffled along; their ankles bound as well as their minds. Marshall sat next to the pilot holding a gun pointed at the first two securely bound jihadists, Miguel and Rebecca. Hansen was in the hold behind Joel and Agnes, armed with a side arm. The unwelcome guests were bound and gagged for the duration of the flight.

On arriving at the island, the pilot set the helicopter down next to a freshwater lake with a copse of fruit-bearing trees nearby. Each prisoner was placed, bound and gagged, fifty yards apart. Marshall said, "You will find a way to release one another. There is water close by. In the pack placed by the lake, there is food to see you through the next few days. At this spot, tomorrow, we will drop further rations and tools."

Then he surprised them with an expression learned recently from Hansen. *"Asalaamu Alikum Wa Rahmatulah Wa Barakatuh."* The prisoners looked at him with total astonishment. He had said to them, "May the Peace and Mercy of Allah be upon you."

That evening, the council gathering of the pioneers at Oasis village took place. Hansen asked Edith to ensure that their views had not been shattered. She reminded them of the firm strategy for being here on the new planet.

"It is our sacred duty to create and foster a caring, sharing community and apply that in equal manner to the environment we are blessed with. This is the base ethic for being here. Humanity's existence on Earth did not follow these ethics as economic dynasties overrode all other concerns for the poor, destitute and vulnerable. So I express once more what we must stay true to:

Get rid of individualism and greed.

Hold dear our connections as human beings.

Reject self-centeredness and self-absorption.

Truly take care for our brothers, sisters and nature."

There was deep silence, agreement and embraces amongst the pioneers.


One week later, Marshall took the precautionary measure of sending a drone over the island where the jihadists had been left.

He saw on the live stream of data that one woman had been hung from a tree by the lake. The bodies of two others lay inert nearby. The final body was located close by. When he grimly reported this to the Community council, there was no rejoicing at the implosion by the sleeper jihadists, just the realization that their own community had acted in good faith with their enemies.

There was a further helicopter journey to bury the four bodies. Hansen had a copy of the Qur'an, which he held in his hand. He read the appropriate verses for burial and stood with Marshall by the four graves.

After a moment of silent prayer they collected the spades that dug the graves and returned to their pioneer community

# Publications - The Author's Works

To the best of my ability, I endeavor to follow Gandhi's principles of *ahimsa* (do not harm) and the teachings on mindfulness. These are the guidelines and foundations for my peace and environmental activism. I live very simply as a planetary activist, Zen teacher, and recognized guru in India. My initial task is to refine my own consciousness - to be a vehicle to chart an authentic path. The focus on daily mindfulness enables me to be still and clear. My passion for the preservation of Mother Earth propels me to serve the planet and humanity by creating bridges and pathways of mindfulness for community activism. Over the past fifty years I've penned 18 books. The literary journey continues with this collection of Short Stories – a new phase for my pen. My hope is to get your attention.

I have transformed several writings from my prior books to cast a sharper short story more suitable to this collection. Also, *Four Arrows* was featured in Ariel Chart Literary Journal, *Love Lost and Dark Shadows* appeared in a radically different form in an Ottawa Independent Writers anthology. *Astrophysics and Parallel Universes* is a rewrite from Michel Weatherall's 2020 anthology titled *Thin Places*. I thank respective editors Mark Rossi, Bob Barclay and Michel Weatherall for their belief in my work.

* New Directions in Economic Anthropology.
       Special Edition of the Canadian Review of Sociology and Anthropology, 1973
* Reflections: The Anthropological Muse
       American Anthropological Association, 1985
* Leadership and Ethics
       RSVK India, May 1997
* Anthropology at the Edge: Essays on Culture, Symbol and Consciousness / University Press of America, 1997

* The Essential Spiral: Ecology and Consciousness After 9/11
        University Press of America, 2002
* Failsafe: Saving the Earth From Ourselves
        Manor House Publishing, 2008
* Earth My Body, Water My Blood
        Baico Publishing Inc, 2011
* Song of Silence
        Baico Publishing Inc, 2011
* Portals and Passages: Book 1 and Book 2
        eBooks on Amazon.com Kindle, 2012
* Keeping Dharma Alive: Volume 1 and Volume 2
        eBooks on Amazon.com Kindle, 2012
* Redemption
        Xlibris LLC, 2014
* Trailing Sky Six Feathers: One Man's Journey with His Muse
        Xlibris LLC, 2014
* New Planet New World
        Manor House Publishing, 2016
* Painting With Words: Poetry for a New Era
        Manor House Publishing, 2018
* Shattered Earth: Approaching Extinction
        Manor House Publishing, 2019
* Past, Present and Future: Stories that Haunt
        Manor House Publishing, 2021
* 2 CD's and 2 DVD's
* 4 films
* 8 Professional Honors, 5 book awards
* 10 Scientific and Technical reports
* 100 professional articles/chapters/book reviews published
* 26 Electronic television courses broadcast at Carleton University and TVO
* 50 articles in Pine Gate – Online Buddhist Journal; 200 articles in newspapers

# ABOUT THE AUTHOR

Dr. Ian Prattis, Professor Emeritus at Carleton University in Ottawa, Canada, is an award-winning author of eighteen books.

Recent awards include Gold for *Redemption* at the 2015 Florida Book Festival, 2015 Quill Award from Focus on Women Magazine for *Trailing Sky Six Feathers* and Silver for Environment from the 2014 Living Now Literary Awards for *Failsafe; Saving the Earth From Ourselves*. He received the 2019 Gold from the eLit Excellence Awards, the 2011 Ottawa Earth Day Environment Award and in 2018 the Yellow Lotus award from the Vesak Project for spiritual guidance and teaching dharma. His book *"Shattered Earth"* received the 2020 Gold Medal from the eLit Excellence Awards.

Born on October 16, 1942, in Great Britain, he notes: "I grew up in Corby, a tough steel town populated by Scots in the heartland of England's countryside. Cultural interface was an early and continuing influence. I was an outstanding athlete and scholar at school, graduating with distinctions in all subjects, but did not stay to collect graduating honors, as at 17 years old I travelled to Sarawak, Borneo with Voluntary Service Overseas (1960 - 62) – Britain's Peace Corps. I loved the immersion in the cultures of Sarawak and was greatly amused by the British colonial mentality, which I didn't share. I was embarrassed to be written up in the home press as "Boy Explorer Discovers Central Borneo!" I had not discovered anything; Kayan tribesmen had taken me there. I had an acute sensitivity and respect for other cultures and traditions, and knew I was privileged to be with skilled guides."

"Returning to Great Britain was an uneasy transition," he recalls, "though I did manage to get an undergraduate degree in anthropology at University College, London (1962-65), before continuing with graduate studies at Balliol College, Oxford (1965-67). At Oxford, academics took a back seat to the judo dojo, rugby field, bridge table, and the founding of irreverent societies at Balliol College. Yet by the time I pursued doctoral studies at the University of British Columbia (1967-70), my brain was switched on. I renewed my passion for other cultures, researching North-West fishing communities within a mathematical, experimental domain that the discipline of anthropology wasn't ready for. Being at the edge of new endeavors was natural and continues to be so."

"I was a Professor of Anthropology and Religion at Carleton University in Ottawa from 1970 to 2007," he notes. "Fieldwork amongst North West Coast American aboriginal populations and North Atlantic fishing communities was an early focus. An interest in Indigenous land claims led to ongoing fieldwork in Indian and Inuit communities, with an emphasis on training native leaders to conduct their own research process. I have worked with diverse populations all over the world and have a passion for doing anthropology. It's better than having a real job - everything changes and the only limits are my imagination and self-discipline."

"My career trajectory has curved through mathematical models, development studies, hermeneutics, poetics and symbolic anthropology, to new science and consciousness studies. The intent was always to expand, and then cross, existing boundaries, to renew the freshness of the anthropological endeavour and make the discipline relevant to the individuals and cultures it touches. My highly acclaimed television course on "Culture and Symbols" drew on these perspectives," he adds.

"The millennium project for the year 2000 created another twelve part television course on "Ecology and Culture," he notes. "I studied Tibetan Buddhism with Lama Tarchin in the early 1980's, Christian meditation with the Benedictines, and was trained by Native American medicine people and shamans in their healing practices and I also studied the Vedic tradition of *Siddha Samadhi Yoga,* and taught this tradition of mediation in India (1996–1997) and was ordained as a teacher and initiator – the first Westerner to receive this privilege."

He adds: "I was recognized in India as a guru – *Prem Chaitania.* Since meeting Thich Nhat Hanh, the Vietnamese Zen Buddhist master, I found a way to take my experiences much deeper after receiving the Lamp Transmission from Thich Nhat Hanh. "

"I have trained with Masters in Buddhist, Vedic and Shamanic traditions and encourage people to find their true nature, so that humanity and the world may be renewed. I have taught children's meditation courses as well as adult and advanced retreats from coast to coast in Canada. I have travelled widely on this beautiful planet to give talks and retreats in Canada, India, Europe, the USA and South America. The basic commitment I hold is to make the world a beautiful place by encouraging people to embrace their true nature."

Outlining another initiative, Dr. Prattis notes: "At the outbreak of the Iraq war I founded Friends for Peace Canada - a coalition of meditation, peace, activist and environmental groups to work for peace, planetary care and social justice. I was also the editor of an online Buddhist Journal and the resident Zen teacher of a meditation community," adds Dr. Prattis, who also writes poetry, including *Reflections: The Anthropological Muse* (1985) and *Painting with Words: Poetry for a New Era* (2018, Manor House).

"The Zen teacher is not separate from the professor or the global citizen," Dr. Prattis notes: "I have six children and fourteen grandchildren from my first marriage. Later in life, as a respite, I lived in a hermitage in Kingsmere, Quebec, in the middle of Gatineau Park forest when my pet wolf was alive. My interests include cross-country skiing, hiking, canoeing and caring for the world of nature. I also enjoy Qi-Gong, gardening, playing baseball and swimming with dolphins."

"I now live with my present wife, Carolyn, in the west end of Ottawa, and stay mostly local to help turn the tide in my home city so that good things begin to happen spontaneously," he adds. "My poetry, memoirs, fiction, articles, blogs and podcasts appear in a wide range of venues. I believe that beneath the polished urban facade remains a part of human nature that few acknowledge, because it is easier to deny the basic instincts that have kept us alive on an unforgiving earth. I choose to go there - a stone tossed into the waters of life."

Manor House
www.manor-house-publishing.com